Dark Tales

of

TERROR

Edited By Michael Knost

Woodland Press, LLC

Copyright © 2010 Woodland Press, LLC
ISBN 978-0-9824939-6-0

All rights reserved. Written permission must be secured from the publisher to use or reproduce any part of this book in any form or by any means—graphic, electronic, or mechanical, including photocopying, recording, taping, or by any information storage retrieval system—except for brief quotations in critical reviews or articles.

Published by
Woodland Press, LLC
Chapmanville, West Virginia • USA
www.woodlandpress.com

SAN: 254-9999

III

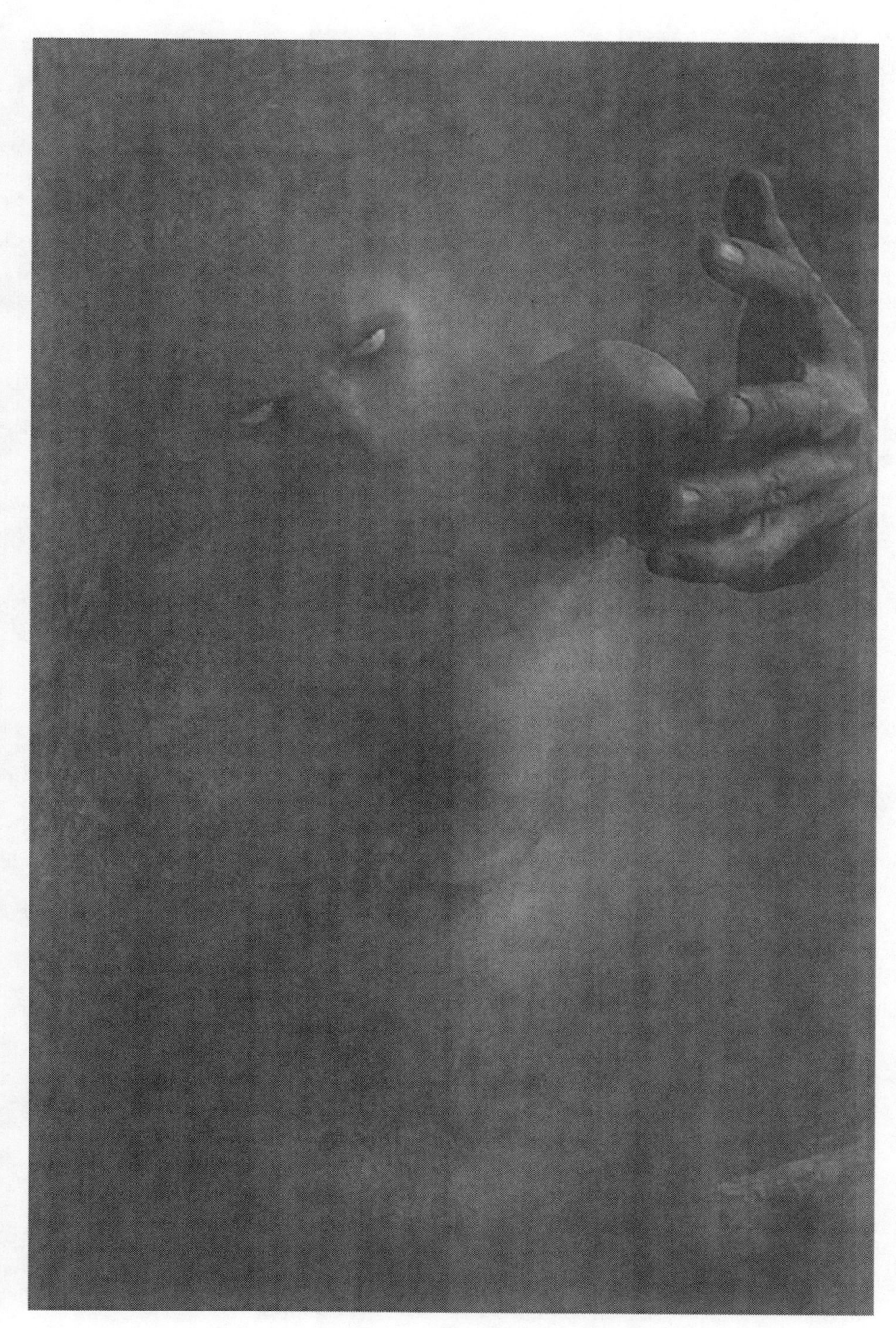

Introduction

My fascination with scary stuff is rooted in the foothills and mountains of southern West Virginia. I recall drinking in the ghost stories and legends surrounding the coalfields and hollows from an early age. It seemed everyone I knew had his own particular twist on these familiar tales. These were folks you would never dream would've had an interest in paranormal activity or the macabre. They were simple, hardworking people. Maybe that's why their stories always riveted me—the tellers were reliable sources, from my point of view.

Well, that's exactly what I wanted to accomplish in this anthology—a collection of stories from reliable sources. Now, don't get me wrong ... what you are about to read are all fictional tales; however, the writers of these yarns are reliable in bringing you that magical element known as "suspension of disbelief."

To accomplish my goal, I sought writers from my home—the wild, wonderful state of West Virginia. Every author in this anthology has a distinct connection to the Mountain State. The neat thing about this project is the level of skill you find from contributor to contributor: some are professionals earning a living from the craft, while others are hobbyists or up-and-comers. The stories are wide-ranging, with a variety of textures—*but all are exceptional.*

I remember my grandmother explaining to me, when I was just a young boy, about the craft of creating her heirloom quality handmade quilts—how the best quilts were those made from both new and old materials, and that each element, with its differences, had its place in the finished product. Not only were her unique creations beautiful, but warm and soft—a treasure to the owner.

Here's hoping you will treasure the patchwork of ghostly stories in this anthology, finding them strangely comfortable—in an eerie sort of way—as well.

— **Michael Knost**

Table of Contents

Threnody
    G. Cameron Fuller — Page 1

Can't See the Forest for the Trees
    Karen L. Newman — Page 14

Thinning the Herd
    Michael Knost — Page 21

The Sepulcher of New Suns
    Brian J. Hatcher — Page 38

The Chief
    Michael Fitzgerald — Page 49

Walking the Path
    Lesley Conner — Page 57

Here Be Demons
    Karin Fuller — Page 63

Fleshman Cabin #6
    Ellen Thompson McCloud — Page 68

The Sweet Song of Canaries at Midnight
    Jude-Marie Green — Page 80

A Matter of Spoons
      S. Clayton Rhodes   Page 86

Shy One Pearl
      Robert W. Walker   Page 95

Nigh
      Eric Fritzius   Page 102

Jackson Gainer's Ghost
      Ellen Bolt   Page 106

Never After
      Jessie Grayson   Page 113

It's Failing Time
      Miranda Phillips Walker   Page 124

Deep River
      Jason L. Keene   Page 133

Other Great Book Titles
From Woodland Press, LLC

Legends of the Mountain State
Volumes 1 - 3 *(and coming soon, volume 4)*
Ghostly Tales from the State of West Virginia
Edited by Michael Knost

Writers Workshop of Horror
Edited by Michael Knost

Appalachian Winter Hauntings
Edited by Michael Knost and Mark Justice

The Secret Life and Brutal Death of Mamie Thurman
By F. Keith Davis

West Virginia Tough Boys
By F. Keith Davis

The Tale of the Devil
By Dr. Coleman C. Hatfield and Robert Spence

The Feuding Hatfields & McCoys
By Dr. Coleman C. Hatfield and F. Keith Davis

ARCH: The Life of Governor Arch A. Moore, Jr.
By Brad Crouser

Appalachian Case Study: UFO Sightings, Alien Encounters, & Unexplained Phenomena, Volumes 1 and 2
By Kyle Lovern

w w w . w o o d l a n d p r e s s . c o m

Threnody
G. Cameron Fuller

G. Cameron Fuller lives in South Charleston, West Virginia. He and his wife, Karin, the unnamed co-author of all that he writes, are raising a 12-year-old until she is far enough off the ground to drop. They hope she won't make too much of a fuss when that happens. In the meantime, he is working on a horror novella and a true crime book.

So accustomed was Donovan to his unscented world that when his nostrils were assaulted by the pungent aroma of flowers, he staggered, his back jerking straight like he was a marionette. He'd never felt anything like that. His face lifted to the mall balcony above, his prominent nose and cavernous nostrils twitching. Intrigued, he abandoned his place in the Starbucks line so he could track down its source.

For most of Donovan's 29 years, he'd endured jokes about his big nose. Classmates and coworkers pretended to use it for shade. He'd been asked if it had its own zip code. Received more than one gag gift of a grindstone. He always laughed as if he'd never heard *that* one before. What no one knew, though, was that in spite of its size, his smeller was far less effective than most. His many childhood allergies had led to years of prescription nasal sprays, effectively deadening his sense of smell.

Donovan stood with slack arms, slowly swiveling his head like a tracking antenna. This was the wrong time of year for flowers, already a couple of hard frosts, even one early snow, but that smell had been flowers, and Donovan was determined to find its source. To his right was the escalator. He started walking.

Like a bloodhound, Donovan trailed his prey, uncertain who in the crowd on the Up escalator was responsible for the odor he was finding so very pleasant, and so immensely disturbing. As they reached the top, people peeled away until there was no one left but a tiny old lady bent like a question mark over her cane. Donovan watched as the fragrant woman scurry-shuffled toward the Court Street exit. For someone so obviously ancient, she was making good time as she maneuvered through the smokers posted like guards just outside the mall doors.

Donovan expected that someone as pungent as her would've turned a few heads, but no one seemed to notice. He edged closer, following her out onto the street, the autumn sky white overhead. Not wanting to risk frightening her, he stayed far enough back that, at times, he was a good half-block behind. Still, even that distance didn't much dispel the scent.

Aside from cat urine, the woman's flowery aroma was the first odor Donovan had smelled in years.

After a few blocks, she slowed; she'd reached her destination. The Eikenberry Funeral Home. Donovan watched as a brittle man with stiff hair held open the door for the tiny, aromatic woman. Then, she was gone.

What was that? Donovan thought. *Jeez, now I'm stalking the aged. Am I that desperate for company?*

He shook his head, clearing his mental Etch-A-Sketch, and headed for home. If he hurried, he could still make it in time for Jeopardy. Donovan never missed Jeopardy. Missing it would be bad. If he missed it, he wouldn't let himself watch Entertainment Tonight. That was his rule. One smart show earned him one stupid.

***

A week passed before it happened again, only this time, Donavan was *in* the Eikenberry Funeral Home when he detected the scent.

A young coworker had inexplicably dropped dead at his desk, and Donovan had come to pay his respects. He'd worried there wouldn't be much of a turnout. Although he and Monty hadn't exactly been friends, they'd stood and talked at the vending machines a few times. Like Donovan, he'd been an only child, had few friends, and spent most of his time alone. He'd pictured Monty's parents standing by their friendless son's coffin for hours. The thought wouldn't stop nagging at him.

Those who have no one to mourn them are irretrievably lost.

While most people feared death, Donovan feared even more that someday, there'd be no one grieving for him, that he'd be irretrievably lost. He decided to attend Monty's viewing.

Donovan had only been there a few minutes when his nose started to tingle. He smelled her before he saw her. She was signing the guest book. She paused and removed one of the folded "In Memory" cards. She read the verse, held it briefly to her lips, then tucked it into her purse. With small shuffling steps, quick and quiet, she made her way to the casket, where she crossed herself and knelt briefly, head bowed. When she stood again, one white-gloved hand steadied the casket's edge. She dabbed her eyes with a lacy handkerchief.

Then she turned and looked straight at Donovan. Right in the eye.

Donovan's back jerked straight, as it had that day he'd first smelled her at the mall. She held his gaze; he felt awkward and looked away. When he looked up again, she was focused again on Monty and appeared to be squeezing his hand.

Monty's parents stepped forward to greet her, and after speaking with them for a moment, she embraced his mother and held her for a very long time. Monty's mother seemed to crumble into the old woman, her shoulders shaking with sobs. They began swaying, rocking back and forth, the old woman gently stroking the younger woman's hair.

When the two finally separated, the old woman reached for Monty's father and embraced him as well. Like Monty's mother, his dad seemed to collapse into the old woman's arms, and she held him even longer than she had his wife. If the funeral director hadn't approached, Donovan suspected she would've embraced him much longer, but the director touched the old woman's arm and said something about her not wanting to miss the last bus of the night.

She touched the mom's hand and the dad's arm one last time—then looked Donovan in the eye—and left.

Although they were speaking in low voices, Donovan could hear Monty's parents wondering out loud what her connection was to their son.

Kindergarten teacher? Sunday school?

So familiar—I know I've seen her before.

Up until now, Donovan had led an unremarkable life. Aside from his large nose, everything about him was generic. All through school, he'd never been better or worse than a C student. He'd been a mediocre athlete, an indistinguishable member of the trumpet section (third chair out of six), a fixture in the school library even though he didn't read much. As an employee, he was dependable and competent. He did what he was asked, but no more.

Donovan found his ordinariness comforting. He cherished routine. These odd encounters with the fragrant lady had him feeling on edge, unsettled.

What I really want to know is how many flowers had to die for her to smell so pungent.

***

That night, Donovan couldn't sleep. A cold October wind whirled outside the windows of his second-story apartment. He lay in bed, staring up into the darkness, going over the ritualistic steps that composed his nightly routine. While some might say he bordered on obsessive-compulsive, Donovan thought of himself more as a creature of habit. His routines calmed him, and his world was efficient. Sleep usually came easily, as long as everything was in its place. But the old woman . . .

She seemed to know me. How?

Lying awake for an eternity, Donovan began to think maybe he'd recognized her, too. From when he was a kid.

He thought about roaming the neighborhood as a child, making trails through the woods behind his family's home, building dams in the creek, throwing rocks at the water tower. His family had lived halfway down 21st, a great street to live on if you were a kid: big yards for kickball, a Ben Franklin 5&10 cent store at one end and Ridenour Lake at the other. But there was the one house parents warned their kids to avoid—the last one on the street, set off more to itself than the rest. The small house had faded pink shutters with half-moons cut in them, an overgrown yard and a handwritten "No Solicitors!" sign.

The house looked abandoned, but sometimes at night, you'd see lights. All the kids in the neighborhood said a witch lived there. They said she collected shadows, and if you saw her outside, she always had more than one. On Halloween, they'd dare each other to knock on the door. One time, when Donovan was seven, he did.

And now he remembered.

As he realized this, another memory exploded in his mind, a fragment from his father's funeral. Hershel, a plant worker at Union Carbide, had been killed in a fall at the plant. It happened on Donovan's eighth birthday. At the funeral, he hadn't wanted to approach the open casket and his mother tried to make him, tugging at his wrist, but Donovan couldn't take his eyes off the casket. More correctly, he couldn't take his eyes off the old woman standing beside it, bent like a question mark. She appeared to be holding his dead father's hand.

He'd glanced at the floor. And saw her shadows.

He felt suddenly cold. When he looked up at the woman, she was looking at him. Her eyes locked with his.

She knew him.

***

Their third encounter—or was it the fourth? — happened on the bus a week later. Donovan seldom traveled by bus, but his beloved Civic had suffered a series of expensive illnesses before finally kicking the bucket. He hated not having a car, but he was a sensible man, practical. *Why waste more money on a rust-bucket?* He'd suck it up and ride the bus for a while, save his dough. Buy something good.

The bus was halfway to his stop when he saw her get on. She took the front seat. He was all the way in the back. He could still smell her, every bit as strong as before. The bus was crowded, but through the next several stops, no one appeared to notice her scent. When they reached the corner by Eikenberry, she used her cane handle to snag the cord, signaling the driver to stop.

The bus stopped with a wooosh of air brakes. She stood, but before moving to the aisle, looked back at Donovan. Her voice clear and strong, she spoke with a trace of Irish lilt: "You coming?"

Donovan was on his way to work and needed to stop at the Morning Brew and get his daily coffee and two bran muffins—bagged separately—on his way in, then he had to put one of those bran muffins in Aqualung's shopping cart while the old panhandler pretended not to notice. He hadn't varied his routine in years. Still, he stood and followed the old woman off the bus.

"Come," she said, her cool hand on his forearm. Her head didn't even reach his shoulder, and the powerful scent of flowers filled his nostrils. Together they waited to cross to the Eikenberry Funeral Home. The bus pulled into traffic and cars streamed past as they stood at the corner. Uncomfortable with the silence, Donovan broke it.

"How do you know me?"

She spoke without looking up at him. "I'm Bronagh."

Her answer made no sense to him, but Donovan said, "So you're Irish?" because he couldn't think of any other thing to say.

"Celt," she said. "Are you aware that long ago, they used to pay mourners to attend funerals? Mostly women. They didn't just weep and wail, they also coordinated the services, almost like a conductor. It was a calling more than a profession."

Donovan didn't know what to say. Was she telling him she was a professional mourner? He barely noticed that the cars had stopped for the light.

"Step lively now, Donovan," she said. He would've expected her to lean on him, but she tugged his arm, leading the way across the intersection. "What few people know is that Death needs mourners. Just like God needs worshippers. And years of practice make some people especially good at it."

She led him to the right, pausing in front of the funeral home.

Donovan saw the brittle man with stiff hair holding open the door, then he turned and looked down the street, toward his office.

"I've got to..." He felt embarrassed, ashamed even. The old woman shook her head, looked at the sidewalk. Donovan followed her gaze. Saw her shadows.

"Maybe next time," he said.

He turned abruptly, pulling his arm out of her grip. It felt like he was tearing himself away. Walking fast, almost jogging, he headed for the Morning Brew to get what he needed to meet his self-imposed daily obligation to Aqualung before going in to the office. He had no time for funerals.

***

She knew his name.

After his latest encounter with the old woman, Donovan had lain awake for hours before he finally remembered the small detail that had been out of place. The whole conversation had been so odd, with the talk of mourners and callings, that it had taken him a while to put his finger on the center of the strangeness: She had known his name.

And now, with the end of October drawing near, he lay in bed and listened to the cold winds swirl, tree branches scratch the window glass. The old house creaked and swayed. The house his apartment was in didn't feel like shelter so much as a stack of cards waiting to fall in around him. In fact, his life felt like that now, his carefully constructed order threatened. Now that the old woman had invaded his life.

She knew his name, and lying awake into the night, he couldn't shake the feeling that she was just outside his window, scratching to get in.

***

By the fourth week of October, Donovan caught the bus seconds before it pulled away from the stop. He had always been early, plenty of time to snag his coffee and muffins before the bus arrived, but this morning, he'd been too out of sorts.

His life was unraveling, his systems falling apart. He felt alone and powerless to stop it. He moved numbly through his day, doing the bare minimum, feeling incapable of taking on tasks that required much thought.

After work, he rode the bus aimlessly for hours, as he'd begun to do every night, until he could muster the will to make his way home. His old, safe regimen in tatters, he had no idea what he was doing, until one evening he realized he'd been looking for her. He hadn't seen her for almost two weeks, since he had turned down her invitation to the funeral. He had to find the old woman. He needed to apologize.

When the bus stopped in Nitro, the town Donovan had grown up in, he realized where he was headed. Twenty-first street. The dead end. The old house with pink shutters.

He got off the bus and began walking. It was just past six and nearly dark out. He hunched his shoulders and pulled the collar of his jacket up around his neck. *It was getting cold fast this year*.

He walked briskly up the street. He hadn't been here since his mother had died a decade ago. He passed his old high school—now a neighborhood center—and glanced over at the antique mall that had moved in when the Ben Franklin closed. Moving onto the residential part of 21st Street, he tried to remember the names of the people who had once lived there. Knapp. Ingram. Tauscher. Graves. Medford. And then, there it was.

He paused at the walkway that led to the old house. Only the barest of paths was visible through the tangle of weeds and thorny undergrowth that made up the yard. No lights were on.

Donovan forced himself into motion, wove up the path, knocked on the door. He heard movement inside. His heart quickened. The door opened at last, and in spite of his expectation of darkness, bright light flooded out. At first he could only see her silhouette.

"Trick or treat?" she said, then she laughed. Until that moment, Donovan hadn't realized it was Halloween. She stepped back and gestured. "Come in, Donagh."

He went in.

It was nothing like he imagined. For a woman who looked so tidy and neat, her house was a mess. Newspapers piled everywhere, as high as his shoulder, a path through them branched off to the right—the kitchen, probably—and another path led straight back, presumably to the bedrooms. Many of the houses in the neighborhood were identical.

She led him to the right, and sure enough, the path opened to a kitchen. This room was warm and clean and smelled of baking bread.

"Sit, sit," she said, pointing toward the small kitchen table and its two chairs. On the table were three newspapers and a couple of photographs. "I was hoping you'd come tonight."

"Does anyone . . ." He looked around. "Do you get many trick-or-treaters?"

"Only you," she said.

She laughed. It was a nice laugh, not a witch-like cackle at all.

Maybe it was the environment, here in her own house, but she looked much younger, stood straighter. It seemed to him she had fewer lines etched in her face. It was softer somehow.

"Sit," she said again. "The tea will be ready in a sec. You might like to look at those."

The first was a thick scrapbook with black paper pages that were beginning to crumble with age. Attached one to a page were *In Memory* cards.

In affectionate remembrance of William, beloved husband of Sarah McIntyre, who entered into rest March 22nd, 1913, in the 71st year of his age.

Donovan flipped through the album, which spanned a three-year period, from 1913 to 1916, then picked up the album beneath it.

"I think the one you have there is from 1903," she said. "That one year filled a whole book. They say West Virginia's never suffered a plague, but you look at the dates on those cards and tell me there wasn't an epidemic of some sort going on."

As he paged through the book, Donovan skimmed the text on the cards. One was for three members of the same family who were being buried on the same day, their listed "Day of Passing" each one day apart.

Donovan closed the book and slid it on top of the first, then pulled out the one at the bottom. On its cover were the words, "They who have none to grieve them are irretrievably lost. Blessed are they that mourn."

Most of the pages of this album were filled with handwritten entries and only the occasional card. Near the back, tucked between the pages, was a photograph of three people standing in front of a church. One, by his clothing, appeared to be a minister. Next to him was a tall, but stoop-shouldered old man. He had sad eyes and an extraordinarily large nose. Beside him was a little old lady, bent like a question mark over her cane.

Aside from her clothes, she looked the same then as now.

The date on the picture was 1881.

Donovan stared at the picture, his brow furrowed.

"Trying to do the math, aren't you?" She chuckled. Handing Donovan his cup of tea, she eased into the chair opposite him. "I'm an old one,

Donagh. Let's just leave it at that."

"Why do you keep calling me that?"

She shrugged. "It's close to Donovan. It was your great-great-great grandfather's name. The last real Celtic name in our family."

"*Our* family?"

She put her small, cool hand on his. "I know I told you that most professional mourners are women, but they don't have to be female. More a matter of temperament."

"Wait," Donovan said. "Explain what you meant by *our* family."

"Hershel was my great-great-great-great-great grandson."

"My father?" Donovan's dad had said he had no family, that he'd been orphaned as a teen and was the only one left.

She nodded. "The first Donagh was my son. He was the first generation born on this continent. You look just like him."

"That's not possible."

"That doesn't happen every day, I can tell you that," she said, reaching across and tapping his nose. "The spittin' image. As soon as I saw you at your father's funeral, I knew you were the one. That I wouldn't have to be doing this alone anymore."

She leaned over and hugged him. He was surprised by how strong she was, and how nice. He couldn't remember the last time he'd been hugged, the last time he'd touched another person beyond a handshake.

"You do realize that you sound like a nutcase," Donovan said.

She laughed. "Let me tell you a story. It happened many years ago. Before we came to this country. Come to think of it, I'm not sure this was even a country yet. I was a girl, no older than fourteen. I can't remember exactly."

She swirled her tea, took a sip. Donovan waited for her to continue.

"A plague took my family, one by one," she said. "A terrible sickness. My uncle was the last to go, and he took the longest. I stayed awake day and night, dabbing him with a wet rag, trying to keep him cool. He lingered so long I began to think he might make it, but then he started coughing up blood, just like the others.

"My family was pretty strong Christians. Not everyone was in those days. My uncle needed a proper funeral, but I was the only family left, so I hired mourners to wail and shriek, to sing sad songs and play their instruments. I was absolutely fascinated by these people, by how genuine their grief seemed to be.

"I was sitting in the pew, watching them, but afraid to look at my uncle's box. I knew I should go up and kneel, say a prayer, but I was afraid. I expect you know that fear." She paused, looked at him, and he nodded. He knew.

"I was averting my eyes from the casket when I noticed a shadow back in the corner behind it, and I suddenly felt cold all over. I knew that shadow. It was Death."

She paused a moment to take another sip of her tea. "Death doesn't look at all like what people think. He's not tall with a hood and a scythe. He's just a shadow standing back by the coffin, waves of gloating sadness pouring from him.

"He's hard to describe," she said. "It's like he's a solid shadow. A shadow only exists in the light, and Death doesn't exist except for life. He's a constant *presence*. Undeniable. Unstoppable. And he looked right at me. He *chose* me. And as I walked back to my empty house that day, I saw I had two shadows. Just like you."

Donovan looked at the floor. She was right.

He jerked side-to-side several times to watch how his shadows moved. *How long had it been there?*

The wind was whipping hard against the house, nearly drowning out the sounds of the laughing trick-or-treaters outside who were likely daring each other to knock on the door.

Donovan thought about Halloween and the thin veil between Life and Death on this one night of the year.

"So you're saying Death picked you that night?" Donovan shook his head. "You're saying Death won't let you die?"

"Not as long as I mourn for others. He needs me. We don't keen and wail like the old days, but professional mourners still exist. And like I said, it's more of a calling than a profession. It's your turn now."

"You're saying you can't die?"

"Oh, I can," she said. "If I stop mourning the dead. My husband got tired of funerals. He'd sit in a washtub for hours trying to get rid of that smell. He couldn't take it any more. He stopped mourning. Not long after that, his shadow swallowed him whole.

"But honestly," she said, "it's not all that bad. You learn what to say, how to comfort. You're providing a service. In return, people hug you and hold your hand. You can feel their gratitude. That's the part I like best. If it weren't for funerals, who would touch an old bag like me?"

She smiled as she reached over and touched his hand. He smelled a burst of cloying flower-scent, the aroma of a thousand dying flowers trapped in a very small funeral home.

"But you know, I'm getting a bit tired myself—not just of the funerals. I'm tired of life. I believe I've simply lost interest, and that's why I was so glad to see you. Now, when it's my time for death, I'll have someone to mourn me. I was so afraid I was going to be irretrievably lost."

She wouldn't be lost. Donovan knew he'd make certain of that. And that awareness made him very afraid.

Can't See the Forest for the Trees
Karen L. Newman

Karen Newman graduated from Marshall University in 1990 with an MS in chemistry and lived in University Heights for several months. Karen's paternal grandmother was born in 1894 in Mason County, WV, where she grew up with a blacksmith father.

"Are we there yet?"

"What is it with you, Katelyn? You've asked me, like, a gazillion times. I know we got a late start, but we should be there before sunset."

"Your buddies change campsites every year, Josh. God knows where they're at. Besides, I need to call home when we get to the lodge. My sister's due any day now."

"Well, it's not *my* fault you forgot your cell. It's not like Jan can't have the baby without you."

Katelyn looked out the window and wondered why she put up with him. She knew his dad was a multimillionaire and her family really needed their money, but Josh's meanness was starting to affect her sanity. She kicked off her dirty sneakers and rubbed feet that still ached from another long shift at Wendy's. Katelyn was tired of both supporting her family and attending nursing school. How she wished her sister's boyfriend hadn't fled at the news of his impending fatherhood and that her dad wasn't disabled.

"Hey, Josh, you passed the lodge."

"Tough. I want to set up camp before dark. Maybe if you're *real* nice I'll let you call tomorrow."

Tears welled up in her eyes. *Calm down. Don't let him see you cry.*

He'll just keep up the torment in front of his rich friends and their snooty girlfriends. Please, God, let me get that ring soon.

They drove down a gravel road that led deep into the forest. Katelyn rolled down the window. The crisp breeze dried her eyes and blew through her chestnut hair. A calico quilt of red, yellow, and orange draped over dark brown poles that towered over a floor of crinkly carpet. Several loud honks startled her. She saw two Cadillac Escalades parked in a clearing off the side of the road. Josh's fraternity brothers, Aaron and Todd, waved them over as their blond-haired, blue-eyed girlfriends, Angela and Lisa, seemed joined at the hip near a weathered picnic table. Sara, Lisa's sister, sat in a lawn chair nearby. Her lower face was hidden by the latest issue of *Cosmopolitan*.

Josh pulled his Lexus next to the SUVs. "Get our stuff," he snapped as he hopped out and greeted Aaron and Todd with backslaps.

Katelyn opened the back hatch and removed the cooler full of beer.

"Need any help?" Angela purred with a hair flip.

"Sure."

"Not!" Angela yelled. She and Lisa burst into laughter.

"So, has Josh popped the question yet?" Angela continued, her hand over her mouth to stifle a giggle.

Katelyn took a deep breath and mustered up her biggest grin. "Should be any day now."

Josh turned around. "Okay, you all. Enough's enough. You both know Katelyn's not marriage material."

Katelyn dropped the cooler. The spilled beer emulated the tears that now poured uninhibited from her eyes.

Aaron and Todd turned, agape, in unison.

"You better pick those up," Josh shouted as he walked toward Katelyn.

"Not marriage material? What am I then?" She balled her hands at her side to keep them from trembling.

"I guess worthless."

The girls snickered and the guys looked down at the ground.

"Besides, you didn't actually think I was ever going to marry some poor girl like you, did you?" Josh said, a glint in his eyes.

"That's not cool, dude," Aaron said. "I'm going home, man."

"But I don't want to," Angela whined.

Aaron shook his head as he picked up the beer cooler. "Whatever."

Katelyn marched to the passenger's side of the Lexus, opened the front door, and grabbed her purse.

"Where do you think you're going?" Josh shouted.

Too mad to say anything, Katelyn swung her purse at the headlights, sending a shower of glass and plastic to the ground.

"You're going to pay for that." Josh said.

"Good luck collecting it. I'm poor, remember." Katelyn ran up the road amid applause.

"You go, girl," Aaron called after her.

What am I going to do? That was my family's last chance for money. Katelyn's only consolation was that the laughter dissipated with each step. She gasped, dizzy. Her chest tightened and her legs became lead ... so heavy she tripped over a tree root and fell. Too tired to move, she laid prone, her body pummeled with waves of sobs. After a few minutes she felt something rough encircle her. She opened her eyes and saw the ground about fifty feet below her. She screamed.

"Be quiet or I'll drop you."

Katelyn looked toward the deep raspy voice. Golden eyes glowed in the dark brown bark of a giant oak tree.

"What's the matter, little girl?" the tree asked. Stick teeth quivered in its uneven mouth.

"My boyfriend used me. I wasted two years of my life for nothing. Where am I going to get that kind of money again?"

The tree's grin widened. "From me."

"How?" She blinked her eyes several times. This had to be a nightmare. Maybe she hit her head on the way down.

"Be my faithful servant."

"What?"

"You see, we trees need nourishment for the winter and our food supply is hard to come by these days. All I need you to do is bring us food during autumn. You can make your own hours as long as the quota is met."

Katelyn couldn't believe her ears. "How?"

"You'll see after sunset. Agree now. It's in your best interest."

She looked down. Could she survive the fall? Probably not. What choice did she really have? "I'll do whatever you say."

"Good." The tree covered her mouth, clasped her hand, and rammed a small sliver of wood under her left thumbnail.

Katelyn squirmed and yelled into its branch-like hand. She almost passed out from the throbbing pain. When she stopped writhing, it placed her back on the ground. "What's that for?" She held up her swollen thumb.

"Insurance. If you don't deliver the quota, the poison now coursing through your body will reach a fatal level by winter. If we're well fed, you'll receive the antidote and a slower reacting poison that will be fatal by the winter after this."

She placed her right hand over the thumb.

"If you try removing it you'll die."

"How long do I have to do this?"

"Wait in that alcove for further instructions." The oak tree indicated a clearing several yards away.

"But—"

The tree's facial features vanished.

"Mr. Tree? Hello?" *Oh my goodness! I made it out of one nightmare into another. Why can't I ever win?* She walked around the tree several times. No face, no voice, no nothing. Katelyn then walked with even heavier feet to the alcove and sat as far away from the trees as possible.

***

After sunset Katelyn heard the raspy voice again. "It's time. Go back to the campsite. Make sure you're not seen."

She jumped up, trembling, and approached the oak. Its eyes were yellow lines.

"Now."

She trotted into the forest. *Crack. Crack. Crunch. Snap.* Sweat rolled down her back as she inched toward the gravel road. She stayed in the shadows, her eyes on the road and her ears toward the voices of her former acquaintances. After what seemed hours, she saw the light from their campfire. She shuffled her feet to minimize noise. When the camp was within sight, Katelyn hid behind a tree.

The wind picked up and drowned out the ghost story Aaron was telling. Fire danced macabre around the marshmallow-tipped sticks they each held. Katelyn's heart sank when Josh snaked his arm around Sara's shoulders.

Katelyn noticed the wind growing stronger and watched as the leaves roiled up from the forest floor. Swirling into six little tornadoes, they bobbled back and forth, teetering like lopsided tops. Inch by inch they approached the campsite. Katelyn followed them from a safe distance.

The first little tornado jumped onto Josh, causing him to scream. He rose from the ground and began spinning like the tops, round and round, faster and faster. At last he tripped over the sleeping bags and onto the fire. Burning flesh tinted the air.

The others stared without moving.

After what seemed hours to Katelyn, Sara squealed like a frightened mouse as she flew up into the air and landed on top of Josh. Their charred flesh fused into a lover's embrace.

The tornadoes spun around camp, sometimes nipping at the campers' feet like puppies, sometimes jumping toward their faces and then pulling back.

"I'm not going to live my life as a cripple," Todd yelled, his eyes wild. He fished a jackknife from his jean pocket and started slitting his wrists.

"Dude, no! Stop!" Aaron bolted toward Todd and slipped onto the dropped knife. The tornadoes, full of sticks and leaves, swirled around both Todd and Aaron. When they withdrew, long bloody gashes covered the men.

Lisa and Angela held each other, sobbing. The tornadoes surrounded them as the fire grew with the wind and covered the girls in a shroud of flames.

Katelyn's breathing was shallow. She shivered at the cool sweat running down her back and leaned against the tree. Then she blinked. She couldn't believe what she saw. White balls bounced on the tornados as they made their way out of camp. She placed a hand over her mouth when she realized the white things were eyeballs. She watched in horror as tree branches plucked the eyes from the air. The wind died down and the leaves fluttered to the ground.

Katelyn ran from the campsite.

"Don't you want your payment?"

She stopped, searching the area. "What are you talking about?" She gasped at the oak that stood only a few feet from her. The other trees walked like crabs on their roots toward her.

"Cash, credit cards, jewels. Take your pick." The oak tree smiled as it sucked on an eyeball.

"What are you doing?" Katelyn's stomach lurched.

"The vitreous humor in these eyes is our sap. Each of us requires about fifty to get through the winter. Sadly these are the first of the season." The oak dropped the now shriveled eye. Katelyn watched it float down to the forest floor like a deflated balloon.

"Your task is to lure people here. We'll do the rest. Now get started. You really don't have much time until winter." The oak lifted its roots and lumbered into the woods.

The campsite started to spin. Katelyn sat with her face in her hands. *I have to get out of here before somebody comes.* She crawled to her knees and stood. She walked over to the girls' purses and took out their cash, thumbing through the large bills. *Must be over two thousand dollars here.* She stuffed the wad in her jeans and approached Aaron.

"You didn't deserve this," she said. "You were by far the best of the bunch." Her fingers twitched. She'd never touched a corpse before. She inched her hand toward his back and plucked out his wallet. She removed the cash and returned it to him. She moved over to Todd. No way was she going to turn him over for the money. Besides, she had enough for now.

She ran to one of the Escalades and smiled at the sight of the keys dangling from the ignition. *Thank God.* She started the engine and drove down the winding gravel road to the lodge. She needed to think of a good story. No one is going to believe her about the tress. She saw a cell phone on the leather seat and picked it up and dialed 9-1-1.

"An attack," she said, through genuine sobs. "A bear attack. My friends have all been killed." Tears streamed down her cheeks. Her heart raced, her chest tightened. She wasn't used to lying.

"No, I don't think there are any survivors." Katelyn hung up the cell phone and threw it out the window. For a second she worried about the GPS, and if the authorities could find her former friends. She stared at her thumb. She had more pressing worries.

Thinning the Herd
Michael Knost

Michael Knost is an award-winning author, editor, and columnist from Chapmanville, WV. He has written books in various genres, edited anthologies such as the LEGENDS OF THE MOUNTAIN STATE series, APPALACHIAN WINTER HAUNTINGS and WRITERS WORKSHOP OF HORROR, which was recently nominated for the Bram Stoker Award. Michael can be found online at www.michaelknost.com.

The Wyoming sky darkened with rain as a chilling wind swept through the plains. Max Carson shifted in the saddle, pulling his jacket's collar together with one hand. He couldn't remember the last time he'd felt the sun on his face.

"Maybe we ought to get back to town, girl," he said, patting the horse's neck. "My rear's gone numb."

The rain stirred an earthy scent, transforming the dirt into reddish mud. Even with the muck, Max loved the peace and quiet of the open plains. No sheriff duties to worry about. No empty house to face. Just ordinary nothingness as far as the eye could see.

He was ready to head back when movement on the horizon caught his attention. The rain and distance made it impossible to make out the figure, yet bristling neck hairs prompted him to rest a hand on his Remington Rolling Block. After losing track of whatever was there, Max ground coarse knuckles into weary eye sockets. *I must be seeing things.*

He pulled out a tarnished flask, downing what remained of the whiskey. The cheap liquor left a trail of warmth in his chest, settling in his gut. Beatrice bought the flask for him as an anniversary gift, yet moved back to Utah six months ago—taking little Emma with her—after accusing him of using the flask more than she'd intended.

Max found the movement again, this time he thought the thing may have been walking upright, yet knew it was too big for a man. But that blob of movement—what little he could see of it—seemed familiar. *Is that a buffalo?* He put away the flask and turned back toward Lander City. "I can't seem to—"

He eased the rifle a few inches from the saddle scabbard before recognizing the approaching rider's red hair. Max often joked about a campfire he'd supposedly set with nothing more than wet kindling and a single strand of deputy William McDougal's hair.

"I figured I'd find you out here," William said, riding closer. "Seeing how tomorrow's such a big day for you."

"You heard, huh?"

"Look, maybe she's coming to patch things up." William sounded as though he was trying to convince himself. "She probably misses you just as bad as you miss her."

"The telegraph said she wants a bill of divorcement, Will."

"Well, that doesn't mean—"

"I appreciate your concern, but I really don't want to talk about it."

William shrugged. "Well, I wanted to let you know a couple of ranchers came by the jail claiming somebody's stealing cattle."

Max rolled his eyes. "Let me guess, they're blaming the Arapaho."

"Actually they say Ben Porter's behind it."

Max laughed. "Ben may be guilty of watering down whiskey but he's no cattle rustler."

William offered a decaying grin. "We'd best be going. We're liable to have the whole town waiting for us."

Max looked back, catching sight of the distant motion again. "Tell me something," he said, nodding toward the movement. "Does that buffalo look peculiar to you?"

Will leaned forward, squinting. "You sure that's a buffalo?"

"Not really." The silhouette disappeared behind rock formations. "But what else could it be?"

"You know, when I was a boy, buffalo ran by the thousands 'round here." Will made a tisking sound. "Hardly see any these days, though."

"That's because the government paid a bunch of men to kill them in order to feed railroad workers."

"There must have been an army of rail hands," William said, gesturing toward the plains. "You couldn't throw a sandstone out there thirty years ago without hitting one of the poor things—buffalo that is, not railroaders."

"Well, as usual, the government didn't give a hoot about feeding railroaders, their goal was to exterminate Indians. They figured it'd be easier to destroy the one thing the natives depended on for everything."

William shook his head. "Buffalo."

"They called it *thinning the herd*, and you can bet your bottom dollar they weren't talking about buffalo."

"You know quite a bit about this."

Max reached for the flask but remembered it was empty. "I was one of the hired guns."

On the way back into town, Max noticed Nathan Jessup and his two sons riding out toward them. Although appearing tall in the saddle, Nathan was smaller than the average rancher.

"Something's got to be done," Nathan said, face red. "I've had two head of cattle stolen in four days."

"Three, Daddy," the older boy said. "Counting this one."

The youngest boy, no older than seven, smiled while twirling a wooden pistol on his index finger. Max wondered if Nathan spent all his time carving toys instead of keeping track of his animals. "Are you sure they're missing? You've got an awfully big place here."

"I know my property, Sheriff!"

Max forced half a smile. "Mind if we look around?"

Cattle grazed in a small valley not far from the bunkhouse. A few hired hands turned toward Max and William as they approached.

"Don't mind us." Max revealed the badge under his jacket. "We're just checking on things."

A light breeze carried the smells of coffee and manure, reminding Max of his early years at his father's ranch. Dick Carson was as tough as Mexican leather and just as unrelenting. But the old man's workers befriended Max, introducing him to his most faithful life companions: plug tobacco and Wild Turkey.

William took a drink from his canteen and handed it to Max. "What do you figure is going on?"

"Hard to say." The canteen's warm water shocked his senses as he'd expected the soothing bite of whiskey. He started to spit it out when something on the hillside caught his attention.

William turned to follow his gaze. "What is it?"

Max pointed to circling vultures on the hillside. "I guess Nathan don't know his property after all."

They headed up the embankment, entering a wooded area where the stench of death lingered like fog near the top. A turkey buzzard took flight from a maggoty mess, startling them.

"Looks like a large calf," William said, pressing a dingy bandana over his mouth and nose.

Blowflies clouded the carcass, buzzing as if a single entity. Max's throat tightened. "I've never laid eyes on claw marks like those."

"Reckon a bear did this?"

Max shrugged. "Whatever did it drug the poor creature here." He pointed out blood specks on broken branches. "Away from the herd."

***

Ben Porter was waiting at the jailhouse when Max and William returned. He'd made himself comfortable, propping his fancy shoes up on the jailer's desk and smoking a fat cigar. "You're running late," he said.

Max hung his hat by the door. "Something I can help you with, Ben?"

"I hear savages killed one of old man Jessup's calves."

Something about Ben reminded Max of his father—both men always made him defensive. "Indians leave nothing to waste," he said louder than intended. "Whatever did this left more than it took."

"You know good and well the savages are just trying to instill fear and confusion."

"I'm telling you, whatever did this was not human."

Ben smirked. "At least we can agree on that."

The front door banged open as young Henry Jessup rushed in. "Sheriff!" The boy grabbed Max's arm. "We can't find my brother Johnny nowhere!"

Ben glared at Max before returning his attention to the boy. "How long has he been missing?"

"Half an hour best we can tell."

Max grabbed his hat. "Let's go, Will."

"I'll round up a few men and—"

"We've got everything under control, Ben."

"Are you out of your mind?" He brushed past Max. "If you're afraid to deal with this, I'm sure we can get the Army to step in and take charge."

"Shouldn't you be at the saloon?" Max said, walking out the door. "You know, handling all the *serious* stuff?"

"Serious stuff?" Ben stepped in front of him. "You mean like listening to drunken lawmen blabbering on about nightmares? Nightmares of buffalo hunting?"

Warmth spread into Max's cheeks. "That's enough."

"But when the hunter gets the buffalo in his sights, just before he squeezes the trigger, the animal takes the shape of a helpless savage child. Then BLAM!"

Max dropped his gaze.

"By the way," Ben said, grasping at Max's pockets. "You'd better make sure your *canteen* is full before you head out!"

Max jerked away, pushing Ben to the side. "I'll handle this," he said, untying his horse.

"You'd better, or I'll have a posse ready by this time tomorrow."

Max and William left the Jessup Ranch with more questions than answers. They'd found no sign of the missing boy so Max decided to visit the Arapaho village.

"I don't think we should do this alone," William said. "Whether the Indians did it or not, they ain't gonna take too kindly to us accusing them."

Former dealings with the Arapaho offered little relief for the cold spot in Max's stomach. "We're not going to accuse them of anything. We're just going to talk to them."

"I hope you know what you're doing."

Overlooking the camp from the hilltop, Max noticed a few scouts using trees and shrubbery as cover. "Well, they've allowed us to come this far."

The natives stared in silence as the two men rode through the village. Max wondered if he could have detected the noiseless crowd had he been blindfolded. As they neared the central portion of the camp, a warrior in chief regalia stepped out from the others. His skin, dark and puffy, his sunken eyes underlined with thick, sagging bags. "What brings the white man to our people?"

Max noticed the scars running from the chief's left ear to mouth and felt the cold spot spread to his chest. "We wanted to warn your people of tragedy."

"Tragedy?" The scars tugged at the man's bottom lip, jerking it with each syllable he spoke.

Max remembered his helplessness the day Emma received her scars. He'd been cutting firewood and was stacking the pieces when her screams reached the woodshed. He followed the cries to a nearby clearing and found the four-year-old pinned down by a massive grizzly.

Before he could move, an Arapaho warrior leaped onto the grizzly's back, stabbing the beast several times with a skinning knife. The bear rose to its hind legs, shrugging the man off like a dog shaking water from its fur. The warrior scurried to his feet and lurched at the bear, drawing its attention away from Emma and Max.

Wasting no time, Max scooped up his daughter and ran for the house. From the edge of the clearing he looked back in time to witness the grizzly slashing at the Indian's face. Max handed Emma to Bea when he entered the house and returned to the clearing with his rifle, finding neither man nor beast, only the crimson remains of their battle.

The scent of curing buffalo hide pulled Max back into the conversation. "Mutilated cattle and missing children," he said. "Some blame a wayward bear."

The chief smiled. "You do not believe this."

"I don't know what to believe."

The chief fixed his gaze on Max and spoke in his native tongue. Before Max could verbalize his ignorance with the Arapaho language, he noticed the crowd disbursing as quietly and purposely as they had gathered.

"Come," the chief said, leading them to a nearby teepee. White smoke escaped the opening flap, dissipating with the breeze. Buffalo furs covered the floor of the teepee except in the center, where remnants of a fire smoldered. "My people call me Akule," the chief said, sitting.

Max lowered himself to the musky hides, briefly meeting William's gaze. "My name is Max Carson. I'm sheriff in these parts." He gestured toward Will. "This is my deputy, William."

Akule took a wooden pipe from a pouch and packed what looked to be tobacco into its stone bowl. "The Skoocoom is restless."

"Skoocoom?"

A plume of smoke rose from the freshly lit pipe, stretching toward the teepee's small opening overhead. "Before our people, there was Skoocoom," he said, handing the pipe to Max. "Our ancestors warned us of the one living in Big Rock Mountain."

Max drew on the pipe, his throat burning from the pungent smoke, a bitter film coating his tongue. "I've never heard of this tribe."

"They are not of our people . . . or others like us." He seemed to be searching for appropriate words. "They were the first people."

Max returned the pipe. "What do you mean *first* people?"

"Before our people, the Scoocoom walked the lands." Akule drew from the pipe again, releasing smoke through his nostrils. "Our people offer buffalo meat to appease the Scoocoom of Big Rock Mountain."

"Appease?"

Akule stared past Max, apparently transfixed on some thought. "The Scoocoom kills our animals and children if we do not appease him."

The wind howled outside, slapping the teepee's hides against its poles. "You talk as though this is some kind of monster."

"Man-bear." Akule returned his gaze to Max. "Few buffalo left. Our people can no longer appease."

"Are you saying this thing is half man and half bear?"

Akule shook his head. "Walk like man . . . look like bear . . . but neither." He raised his hand a few feet above his head. "Great is the Scoocoom, covered in bearskin."

"And it lives in Big Rock Mountain?"

"Many warrior has journeyed to kill the Scoocoom in its cave. None returned."

"Thank you for your time," Max said, preparing to stand.

"Never forget," Akule said, placing a hand on Max's shoulder. "You are the path you take."

"What?"

"Let heart choose path," he said, touching Max's chest. "Then you will be true to self."

***

Max stood on the platform waiting for Bea and Emma's train to arrive. He forced a breath into a cupped hand, sniffing for any hint of liquor. Cringing at the whiskey odor, he bit off a hunk of tobacco and moved it around in his mouth before spitting a stream of amber.

What am I going to say to her?

A distant whistle echoed across the valley, a long wail that almost sounded alive. It reminded him of the train ride to Lander six years ago with Beatrice. The newlyweds had hoped of starting over, leaving his father's abusive expectations behind, as well as her parents' religious traditions.

"What's the latest on the savages?"

Max turned to find Ben walking up the platform. "I told you—"

"Why would you visit them if you didn't think they were responsible?"

Max chomped down on the tobacco, squeezing juice from its core. "I wouldn't be much of a lawman if I didn't check out every possibility, now would I?" He leaned forward, spitting. "What's funny is some of the ranchers named you as a suspect."

"That's not surprising. Most of them owe me money."

The whistle sounded again, louder this time. "Why do you blame the Indians?"

"They're animals." Ben lit a cigar, tendrils of smoke wafting from his head. "It's their nature."

Max focused on the approaching train, breathing in the sweet leathery smoke. "Have you ever heard of a Scoocoom?"

"What?"

He met Ben's gaze. "Never mind."

"I see the savages have filled your head with nonsense, too." He tossed the cigar onto the tracks, stepping closer. "Let me guess, a *man-bear* that kills everything in its path?"

Max lowered his eyebrows. "You've heard of this?"

"Simpleminded fools talk about it in the saloon." He shook his head. "Mostly railroaders who've been influenced by the savages. They think they saw the creature kill a few men."

"But what about—"

"Can't you see what's going on?" The vein in Ben's forehead looked ready to pop. "The savages made all this up to scare us away. And now they're killing our cattle and children to make us think this thing is real!"

The platform shook as the train eased into the station, steam passing over the gathering spectators. "There's more to it than that, Ben, and you know it."

He walked away before Ben could reply, slipping through the crowd toward the train's passenger car. The steam engine gurgled and hissed like a struggling animal just felled by a hunter, its life slowly giving way to the cold.

Several people emerged from the train smiling and laughing as they embraced waiting loved ones. Coldness moved through Max, his heart pounding inside his chest. *Should I hug her*? He brushed dust from his jacket.

"Daddy!" His daughter waved from the steps, Beatrice behind her, expressionless. Emma ran to him, jumping into his arms. "We saw buffalo in the plains," she said. "Real buffalo!"

Max laughed, pulling her close. "How about that, real buffalo!"

Beatrice offered a cold stare as she stepped forward. "Can you get our bags?"

***

Emma played outside as Max watched from the open door. He couldn't believe how much she'd grown in just six months. Her features and quirky movements were familiar, the spitting image of her mother.

"She's missed you."

"And I've missed her," Max said, turning to Bea. "You, too, of course."

She curled her lip into a half-smile. "How much have you had today?"

"What do you mean?"

"Whiskey," she said, no longer smiling. "How much have you had today?"

He shook his head. "I'd rather not—"

"Nothing's changed, has it?"

Max hung his head, pushing away thoughts of his father's lectures on the evils of alcohol and how he'd never amount to anything.

"Are you listening to me?"

He looked up, avoiding eye contact with her. "I just—"

He wasn't sure if he'd actually heard Emma scream; after all, her shrieks had echoed in his woozy head since the attack. He quickly stepped outside, jumping off the porch. "Emma?"

With no answer, he ran to the back of the house, scanning the outlying copse of trees.

Beatrice came up beside him. "Emma!" Her voice was shrill, panicked.

Everything blended with the trees until Max noticed the hulking figure carrying a slumped body into the woods. His chest tightened, his heart struggling to push chilled blood through his veins.

"Oh, my!" Bea's voice was hysterical.

Max grabbed her by the shoulders. "Listen to me! I need you to go into town and get William."

"But, I—"

"There's no time for this, Bea. Just do as I say!"

After getting his rifle, Max ran to the area where he'd last spotted the figure. Although the tracks were humanlike, they were double the size of anything he'd ever seen. For a second, he thought he would vomit, the grimness of the situation more than he could bear.

Following the tracks toward Big Rock Mountain, Max picked up the pace when thoughts of the creature killing Emma en route crossed his mind. *I'm coming, baby!*

His legs grew heavy and painful, his lungs burning like coals of fire. The worst part was trying to breathe, especially amid the stench. The thing smelled like a wet bear in the heat of the day, except its scent was much stronger, muskier. *I haven't forgotten my promise.*

He remembered holding Emma a few weeks after the grizzly incident, realizing for the first time she had far more scars than those visible. She couldn't sleep for more than half an hour at a time, and even then, she'd awaken in tears.

"Will the bear get me in my sleep?" she'd asked.

"No, baby."

"How do you know?"

"Because I'm here to protect you."

"But—"

"I'll always protect you."

"Do you promise?"

He remembered hiding his tears. "I promise."

Guttural cries in the distance set his skin to crawling. Noises from all directions made him wonder what lay ahead. Shivering from his sweat soaked shirt, Max felt as though he'd been running for days, his teeth chattering as he willed himself to keep going.

I promise.

He stopped to catch his breath at the base of the mountain and noticed the enormous rocks jutting from the red dirt like granite teeth protruding from swollen gums.

"Sheriff!"

William came through the brush with Ben Porter following.

"When Beatrice told me what had happened, I knew you would come here," William said from his horse.

Ben dismounted, stuffing a long revolver in his belt. "Tell me how I can help, Sheriff."

Max felt a sense of countenance with Ben at his side. "Get your lantern and come with me up the mountain." He turned to William. "Take your horse and go around the far side, Will. Head up the mountain from there in case the thing tries to escape."

"It won't escape," Will said, lifting his rifle for Max to see. "I promise you that."

***

The mountain was difficult to climb with all the loose dirt and pebbles scattered over the endless granite. But it was perfect for tracking as Max and Ben made their way towards the top.

"I want to apologize for—"

"There's no need," Max said, shaking his head. "You were doing what you thought was best."

Ben held his gaze to the ground. "Yeah, but some of the things I said—"

"It's in the past," Max said, placing a hand on Ben's shoulder. "Let's focus on getting Emma."

"You bet."

Near the top, they discovered a massive cave that resembled a gaping mouth, awaiting prey. The stench emanating from the entrance was so strong Max could have sworn he could see it.

"Do you think it's in there?" Ben asked, taking out a box of matches.

"It has to be."

The bleak light from the lantern illuminated the caves floor only a few feet as they stepped over rocks and debris.

The snapping, crunching under their boots echoed against the rocks, invoking a sickening feeling with every step.

"What is that?" Ben said, holding the lantern closer to the ground.

"Bones."

Ben raised the lantern face level. "Human bones?"

"Buffalo."

He returned the lantern to the floor. "Look at this," he said, retrieving something from the remains. "Looks like a wooden gun."

Max stared at the bloodstains on the carving.

"What's wrong?"

"That belonged to the Jessup boy."

A rumbling growl resonated in the distance, prompting Ben to shift the light in its direction. The lantern's flame flickered from the brisk movement, causing the light to dim to a glowing wick before dying out.

Darkness bit Max through his shirt. "Can you relight it?"

"It will be a while before I can try. It's too hot."

Max squinted at a faint glow in the distance. "What is that?"

"Looks like fire."

Soft light danced against the rock walls as the two men approached a sharp bend in the passageway. The air reeked of the beast, clinging to their clothing and pores. The sounds of crackling fire seemed to be the music the light danced to.

"Hold on a second," Max whispered.

Peeking around the corner, he found a campfire with smoke drifting into ceiling cracks. Emma was on the floor not far from the fire, her eyes closed. *God please let her be asleep.* Something in the shadows caught his attention, the light flickering on an enormous figure squatting in the corner.

He eased his gaze back to Ben, nodding for him to take a peek. "It's near the back wall in the shadows."

"I think it's asleep," Ben whispered.

"Take my rifle," Max said, holding out the Remington, "and give me your pistol." He quickly glanced back at the thing. "I'll try to get Emma without waking it, but if it moves, shoot for its chest."

"All right."

Max tucked the pistol in his belt and eased around the corner, his gaze never straying from the beast. *Please let her just be sleeping.* The snoring from the thing sounded like horse grunts, its massive chest moving in rhythm.

He slowly knelt beside Emma, placing a shaking hand in front of her nose. The warm breaths on his palm brought tears of joy to his eyes. He glanced back at Ben before attempting to lift her. The Scoocoom snorted in its slumber, causing Max to flinch.

Max slipped his hands underneath Emma, trying to get a good hold when her eyes fluttered. He no more got her an inch from the ground when she flailed at him, screaming.

As Max tried to get her quiet, a gunshot startled him, leaving only a high-pitched ringing in his ears. He looked up in time to see the beast rushing towards Ben, its arms poised with bear-like claws ready to strike.

Ben pulled back the hammer on the rifle, rotating the breechblock in an effort to reload, but just as he was ready to aim, the creature knocked him to the ground. The squishing, crunching sounds were maddening, but the gurgling wheezes were more than Max could stand.

The beast rose from the floor in a fluid motion, chewing on something unseen. The stench now carried a hint of iron as blood pooled beneath the pulverized mess that once was Ben Porter.

Emma screamed again, causing the monster to turn toward them. Its fur was matted with gore, its claws shining with blood.

Max reached for the pistol in his belt but realized it was gone. He saw that it had fallen from his belt during the excitement and was lying between them and the creature.

The Scoocoom roared, jutting its head forward like a grizzly warning unlucky trespassers. It bellowed again, its lips pulled back from its enormous teeth.

Max pushed Emma behind him, making himself a shield. "Emma, don't move." He said, focusing on the thing.

"But—"

"It's going to be all right," he said, caressing her arm. "I promise."

The Scoocoom slowly approached, blowing Ben's blood from its snout. Its breaths were low guttural sounds, each fading before the next.

"Stay where you are, Emma," Max said, slowly reaching for the gun. "Everything is going to be fine."

His fingers were inches from the pistol when the creature lashed at him. Pain exploded in his shoulder as he fell to the floor, blood flowing from the lacerations. He rolled onto his back and kicked the lunging creature in the teeth, sending it backward.

He quickly scooped up the revolver and fell back into Emma, raising the pistol in a shaky aim. The Scoocoom was only a few feet away when Max squeezed the trigger. The empty click echoed through the chamber, chilling Max to his core.

He squeezed the trigger again with the same result. This time the monster was so close Max could smell the blood on its breath. Emma put her face into Max's back, screaming.

"I love you, Baby," he said, placing the pistol's muzzle under the creature's chin.

The pistol discharged just as the Scoocoom raised its claws, kicking in Max's hand with a great bang. The monster stumbled back and fell forward, blood gushing from the large rupture in its head.

"Is it dead?" Emma asked, peeking from behind him.

He released a held breath. "I think so, Baby." Shaking, he lifted her into his arms and stepped over the carcass, then past the mauled body of Ben Porter. "I think so."

He stumbled from the cave entrance, falling back against its rock facing and placed Emma on the ground. He touched his burning shoulder, bringing back thickening blood, and instinctively retrieved his flask.

"Are you all right, Daddy?"

"I'm fine," he said, staring at the flask. He shifted his gaze to Emma and tossed the flask inside the cave. "Just fine."

He lifted Emma into his arms, the morning sunshine warming his cheeks. "Let's go home, Baby."

A Sepulcher of New Suns
Brian J. Hatcher

Brian J. Hatcher was born in Beckley, WV, and has lived in the Mountain State for most of his life. He currently lives in Charleston, WV, has published several short stories and poems, and can be found online at his website: www.brianjhatcher.com.

Titanium plates, scavenged from the leftover construction materials and engraved with text using a Dremel tool. Not an easy task, but these plates afford me the best chance that someone might, some day, read these words. My last testament to the human race.

Humanity has endured many Dark Ages. Ultimately, its spirit rose from the darkness. Why should this new Dark Age be any different? The Human Race may overcome its fear of the sky. They might trace their steps into space, following the path that once led them to glory. If so, they must eventually journey to the Moon, where they will find this base and observatory. I suspect by then I will be long dead. Generations may come and go before the human race returns to the stars. However, if my loneliness, my exile from Earth, is to mean anything then I have to believe that all I've seen will be undone, some day. I have to believe.

Then again, this may turn out to be the most elaborate means anyone has ever devised to talk to themselves.

Still, my hopes are bound in these words. To read them means more than leaving the Earth behind. Perhaps fear and superstition, too, will fall away in the wake of Humanity's assent. If that's the case then perhaps my story can finally be known. Perhaps even believed.

I am Dr. Everett Madsen. I don't presume my name will mean anything to future generations. I'm fine with that. I took too much pride in my fame when I had it. I'd be content to know my legacy will eventually pass from the world. In fact, it is my fondest wish. The thought that it might live forever horrifies me more than anything I can imagine.

I have another name, one I neither asked for nor wanted: the Great Satan, Destroyer of Mankind and Enemy of the Faith. Although my so-called blasphemies may pass into the annals of myth, I am no myth. And, regardless of my reputation as the Father of Lies, everything I am about to say is true.

Humanity has believed in evil throughout its history and gave it both a personage and a name. The mantle of the Great Satan was forced upon me because I needed to be kept silent. It is because they feared I would speak the Forbidden Canon. Now I must.

I do not do this lightly. I realize it may sound ridiculous, may go against decades, perhaps even centuries, of belief. It may even seem a bit sinister. Nevertheless, I swear upon my life that it is the truth.

There was a time when the Earth had only one sun. I remember it. I saw it with my own eyes.

You've come so far to get here. All I ask is you come but a little bit farther. Please. Hear my story. It is all I have left.

***

Our former Sun, whose light nurtured the Earth from the dawn of its existence, occupied a corner of space not that far away, in cosmic terms. A little over four light years away from where the Earth is now, in the constellation of Cassiopeia. Centauri AB, the Day Sun and Night Sun, were once just a single pinhole of light among thousands in the night sky. The Sun of our origin is gone now. Only a small dark spot in the sky where that proud star once burned, as if it never existed at all. But it did. I swear it did.

The world where I grew up had no fifteen-month years or a second sun that stole the night away for half the year. I suppose these new suns have a beauty all their own, but I didn't take the time to appreciate it. My eyes were elsewhere, as were those of the rest of the world. We were preoccupied with, *How?*, and by extension, *Why?* Ah, but that was the $25,000 Dollar Question, wasn't it? It became the most important question of my life.

The world changed on May 14th, the fifth month in the Earth's old twelve-month year. At 3:29 AM GMT, something massive, and up to that point undetected, passed between the Earth and the sun. For the first time in history, the Earth plunged into universal night, but only for a few scant seconds. Then, scintillating waves of light washed over the Earth. The effect was similar to the aurora borealis, yet many times brighter. The lights lasted twenty-seven minutes. When they faded away, everything had changed. Beginning with the night sky.

Not a huge change, mind you. Most of the constellations kept their familiar shapes. Arcturus and Altair were out of place, as were a few other stars. And, of course, Centaurus lacked its brightest star. However, these changes could very well have gone unnoticed, except for those of us familiar with the night sky.

That the sun now had a neighbor in the day sky was impossible to miss.

Politicians and religious figures tried to soothe the rising fears of the population while the scientific community leapt to action, seeking the answers the world demanded. Telescopes scanned every inch of the sky. Atomic clocks were checked and double-checked. Every scrap of data was collected, collated, and run through endless computer-generated models. In the end, we could not refute the impossible conclusion that any schoolchild with a cheap telescope could see to be true.

The Earth, along with its moon, had been transported from the Sun and placed into an orbit around Centauri A at a distance conducive to life on Earth. All within a matter of minutes.

And this was impossible. Not even light could make the journey at that speed. But it was more than that. To calculate the optimal orbital path for the Earth, to maintain the proper rotational axis, and to comprehend the dependency on the moon's gravity on the Earth's systems, indicated not only an incalculable power but also an indescribable intellect.

I said we kept asking, *How?* and *Why?* More terrifying was that unspoken question of *Who?* These questions ate away at Humanity like a cancer of the soul. I had no idea how bad it would eventually get. Perhaps I didn't really care. I was afraid, too, but I also saw the opportunity of a lifetime.

Most people don't understand the frustrations of the scientist, especially in the early 21st century. Science had advanced far beyond the limitations of our primitive beginnings. No longer did we ask ourselves what might be possible, but instead tested the strength of our knowledge against the power of our imagination. It truly was a golden age where we felt we could achieve anything, if only allowed to follow our dreams.

However, as it has always been, someone else held the purse strings. Therefore, with our hats in our hands, we hoped to convince those sitting on thrones built upon the sweat of our genius that we had much to offer. We'd beg for crumbs, just for the chance to make even one baby step forward. It rankled me to kowtow to those who wallowed in the mud so that I could reach for the stars. I felt like an adventurous child told by his parents to stay in his own yard. The wings of the human race had been clipped by bean counters and bureaucrats for far too long.

Then the world changed, in more ways than just seasons and suns. Suddenly, all that smugness turned to fear and the bean counters grew desperate for answers. I promised those answers, but on my terms. They quibbled, as they always do. But the world knew my reputation. No one doubted I could deliver on my promises.

Astronomy is, at its heart, looking back in time. The light from distant stars takes years to reach us. From our telescopes, we see not what is but what was. With a powerful enough telescope, one can see far into the past, even to the beginnings of our Universe. For the moment, we could still see the light from our original Sun, but that light had taken four years to reach Centauri AB, and us. The light from May 14th was, at the time I offered my proposal to the US government, still over three years away. With the proper equipment, and at the right time, we could peer back into Earth's past and see what happened on that fateful day. But we only had one chance, and a mere three years to prepare.

I proposed an observatory and space station with an array of optical and radio telescopes built to my specifications. The station would need to be fully manned, since the slightest equipment failure at the critical moment would cost us everything. An earthbound observatory took the risk of inclement weather, and no orbiting satellite would be large enough to contain all the needed equipment and staff. The only option that made sense, I argued, would be a massive observatory built on the moon. The project would be expensive, but I assured NASA the benefits would extend well beyond answering our great question. But if they hedged, our one chance would pass us by.

I built up the urgency and played upon everyone's fears. I admit I took advantage of the situation, but I didn't feel guilty. Humanity would ultimately benefit. To let this opportunity pass by would be a great disservice to the human race. At least, that is what I told myself.

In the end, the purses were open to a degree unprecedented in history. Thus began Project Witness. My Xanadu.

The project was a formidable task, but it was also Mankind's crowning achievement. My crowning achievement. However, the glory was not mine alone. I invited dozens of scientists, engineers, and specialists from nearly every civilized country to contribute to the station. Other governments helped to fund many aspects of the project, although I wasn't as forthcoming with NASA as I could have been with the extent of the additional funding. As long as the money kept coming in, no project lacked anything it required to develop to its fullest potential. Dr. Phyllis Bodwell was on the forefront of self-contained living environments. My moon base would require self-sustaining food, water, and oxygen.

Her work was groundbreaking but nearly abandoned when interest in colonizing the moon waned over the previous two decades. Dr. Stanton Grindel's work in macro hydroponics would allow the base to grow enough food to help sustain a staff of 20 people. In addition, Dr. P'an Yüan created special exercises and equipment specifically to combat the effects of the moon's lower gravitation on the human body. These were only a few of the brilliant minds who contributed to this project. At no other time in history has the greatness of human ingenuity vested itself so strongly.

They were all good people. Decent people. I still feel the pain of losing them.

As soon as there was enough of the base built to allow it, and I had completed my training, I took the first Ares IV rocket up to Project Witness. The base was just a skeleton of what it would finally become, but it surpassed all my dreams. I had come home, for the first time in my life, and I think I had never known true happiness until that very moment.

However, there wasn't much time to play tourist. Although construction had proceeded at breakneck speed and exceeded all expectations, we still had only a few months until the Event and there was much left to do. It was stressful but happy work, and I resolved to make the deadline.

As my attention turned ever skyward, public opinion back on Earth swayed against the project. Two years into the project, NASA Administrator Daryl Baines resigned from his post and President Roger Geist lost his bid for re-election by a landslide. That didn't concern me. The check, as they say, had already cleared.

Others on my staff came to me with their concerns. They had heard things from back home, and many worried we would not be permitted to complete Project Witness. It's just the bean counters waffling again, I said. I told everyone to keep working, not to let petty concerns back on Earth distract us. If we could hold out until after the Event, the momentum would carry us past the controversy. Let the small-minded wallow in the mud, I would tell them. We were reaching for the stars.

I ignored the signs because I was naïve. On Earth, there were wars and rumors of wars, but we were untouchable, safe on our palace on the moon. I never doubted that for a moment, not until my dream finally came crashing down.

The order to evacuate the station arrived two months before the Event. No reason was given, and when I tried to contact NASA, they were evasive at best and dictatorial when I pressed the issue. The retrieval crafts had already been dispatched before we knew we were leaving.

Because of weight restrictions, there wasn't much packing to be done. Circe landers touched down a week after we received our orders. Everyone boarded, and the landers headed back to the Orion III orbiters for their journey back to Earth.

Everyone, of course, except for me.

It would take NASA at least six months to prep a rocket and lander to come after me. By the time NASA realized I had not returned with the others and sent a rocket back for me, the Event would have already occurred. I had supplies to last for many months and understood enough about the base to keep it going. I wasn't worried for myself. I worried about the project, and this would be the only way to save it.

I'm sure the crew and staff thought me mad for staying behind, but I believe they sympathized with my reasons. Whatever they thought, no one told NASA I had not boarded the lander.

It's strange. I thought by staying behind, I was the one taking the risks.

I can't be sure what happened. All I have is the newscasts I received on the base. The reporters grew more cruel and callous in their reporting as time went by. The reports would later be filled with lies, that Project Witness had been a swindle intended to appropriate money from the world governments, that there had been no moon base. Therefore, I can't say how much of what the reports said about the accident was true. Nevertheless, the landers did not reach Earth, and all the scientists and staff aboard had been killed.

The reports said all three ships suffered massive system failures during re-entry. It wouldn't surprise me that something more sinister was involved, most likely engineered by the US government. Transmissions over the next few months made it painfully obvious how much had changed back on Earth. But the world believed me dead, and I thought it better they keep on believing it. I was sure that if anyone came back for me, it would be to kill me. Either way, I would never leave the station again.

There is no limit to Mankind's ability to delude itself, and nothing it won't do to protect what it holds precious. The Earth's relocation had been too much to accept, its implications too staggering to bear. I could see, given a generation or two, that the world could convince itself that May 14th never happened, that the Earth has always orbited ☐ Centauri A. I never thought it could happen while those who knew the light of the old sun still lived and could remember. It didn't take but a few years for the entire world not only to spread the lie, but to believe it with all their hearts. In time, fear replaced memory, science, and religion to became the new faith. Mankind rewrote history with a terrifying efficiency. And they changed me as well. I was reborn in the eyes of the world, first as a conman, then a heretic, and then, finally, as the Great Satan.

I thought of my moon base as Xanadu. I have renamed it Pandemonium. I thought it fitting.

***

It has been five years since I first came to Witness Base. The base's efficient, self-contained system could sustain me another five years, easily. One final legacy from the brave souls who died, because of my dream.

Five years seems much too long. I think, perhaps, I will reroute the scrubbers before I go to sleep tonight. To increase the CO_2 content. It will be a painless death.

And so, my final words to Humanity, engraved on metal plates that will not corrode or tarnish. The remains of my legacy. Do with it what you will. But I'm not quite finished, not yet. Still one last tale to tell before my story, and my life, has ended.

After all, I had to see, didn't I? Observatories on Earth had been destroyed with the coming of the New Order. The only one still watching the sky, the only one who dared, was I. I'd lost so much. I had to know. I may be the only one who ever will.

Everything the telescopes picked up during the Event was recorded to digital media. I doubt much of it will survive long enough to be discovered, so only these words shall bear witness to the final mission of Project Witness. I don't know if anyone will believe it. I'm not sure I do. This is what I discovered.

The object that passed between the Earth and the Sun on May 14th was three vessels, ships of some kind I would suppose, although I couldn't make them out. They were massive, each one nearly half the size of the sun. That's why I could see them. They appeared spheroid shaped, and they radiated some sort of visible energy. They positioned themselves around the sun. The glow about them brightened, and beams of hot blue light radiated from the crafts toward the sun. I didn't notice until I watched the playback, but another beam, much smaller than the other ones, shot out from one of the spheroids. The beam struck what I can only assume to be the Earth. A flash of light appeared, then was gone.

Then, the spheroids busied themselves on the completion of their task.

I cannot begin to understand the intelligence guiding the spheroids. I suspect it would be akin to an insect trying to understand a human. However, I know three facts for sure. They are very advanced, are powerful to a point of god-like, and they require hydrogen in massive quantities. It was what they wanted with our sun. Within moments, the energy beams halted all fusion within the star. They blew out the sun as if it were a candle. Then they siphoned out the hydrogen. According to the base's spectrograph, nothing remains but a volume of helium and a few trace elements. After the spheroids retrieved the last of the hydrogen, they flew away so quickly I could not follow them. Where they went, I will never know.

Had the Earth not been moved, it would surely have been destroyed.

I considered contacting Earth with what I'd seen and risking the consequences. I thought it might change the world for the better if they knew. We are not the center of the universe. And yet, although we may be a small, insignificant part of Creation, I thought Humanity could take comfort, perhaps even pride, in knowing that beings of god-like intelligence and power looked upon the Earth, saw the human race, and felt we were worth saving.

But I didn't try to contact the Earth. It was no longer my home. I'm not sure it ever was.

And I've realized, just now, how wrong I've been all along. I'm no better than the rest of humanity. I trusted in a lie, too. It is preposterous to believe the spheroids saved the Earth because of Humanity. The truth is, they saw a pretty bauble and decided to keep safe a while longer. Humanity never entered into their consideration. Too small and insignificant to notice at all.

I always said it was better to reach for the stars than to wallow in the mud. I thought that made me better than other men, but whether you regard the gutter or the skies, in the end you still come to the same conclusion: Humanity is a petty, paltry thing.

No. No one is coming. No one will ever read these words. Mankind has deluded itself back into the center of the universe. They'll not chance losing that position again. They'll stay where they are, because they believe they are safe. And I know, only I know, that they are not. The spheroids might one day choose Centauri AB. Only next time, they may not bother to move the Earth to safety.

And fear will not end the eternal night, should it return and stay forever.

The Chief
Michael Fitzgerald

Born in the Bronx and raised in New Jersey, Michael T. Fitzgerald has called West Virginia his home since 1974. He lived in Hurricane, WV, in his youth and later attended both WVU and Marshall University. Michael now lives in Huntington, WV, where he writes, acts, and directs. He has produced two feature films shot in the Mountain State: LAST HIT and METH MAN.

I've been hunting since I was six. At first going out and sitting with my father in the early days. Pack Mule Mike he'd call me. I'd haul the equipment so he could get off a quick shot. Later he gave me my own 4-10, and I joined him on the hunt proper. Sometimes he even let me get the first shot in. I really enjoyed those days, just as he did with his father many years before.

But now I hunt alone, looking forward to the quiet times. At my father's deathbed I promised I'd always have a good spot next to me on the hunt for him. So I really never feel alone out there.

I stopped by my grandparent's place on the way out this morning. Even though it was quite early, they were already up and at it. I let Granddad check out my new gun. Though he no longer hunts, he loves to see what's new for the modern hunter. A round of, "back in my day," was soon to follow. But it was always a nice visit and a quick meal.

I pulled out my map and laid it on the table. A coworker, Spike Johnson, offered to let me use his land. I didn't want to waste any good hunting time searching for Spike's place, which consisted of ten acres bordering Chief Cornstalk Wildlife Management Area. The only structure on his lot was a crudely built shack, but it would do for what I needed. It was the start of squirrel season, and I wanted a nice place all to myself.

I choked down some of Grandma's wake-yer-butt-up coffee.

"Heading some place new this year?" Granddad asked.

I was tracing the route with my finger, trying to set it to memory. "Yeah, last year I was almost bumping elbows with other hunters. Arguments about tree stands, deer paths. Not this year."

"Up Route 2 I see," he said. "A bit of a haul."

"Yeah, not too far down though. Maybe 45 minutes to an hour total, if I don't get lost."

Granddad pointed to an area on the map outlined with a red marker. "What's that?"

"That's outside Spike's place. Chief Cornstalk Reserve or such. I guess he wants me to stay on his land, you know, to avoid other hunters."

Granddad sat back, his mood, quite somber. "Not to avoid other hunters, son, to avoid the Chief."

I laughed. "Don't worry, Granddad, I'm legal. Got my license," I said patting my shirt pocket.

"No son, not the game warden, Chief Cornstalk," he said ever so seriously. "He wants you to avoid running into Chief Cornstalk."

"The Chief?"

"I'm not joking with you, boy," he said. "The Chief still looks over his land. He protects what is his."

***

I took a left off State Route 2 onto Crab Creek Road, then glanced over at Spike's sloppily sketched map. I was two miles from the official "Welcome to Chief Cornstalk" sign, and about three miles out to Spike's piece of land. I took a sip out of my travel mug and continued down the road.

I had a laugh remembering Granddad's warnings. I soon turned onto a dirt road that led out to several other plots. As I got closer to my destination, the road became rutted and muddy, the tires spinning occasionally in the muck.

Around three miles down I spotted the worn roof of Spike's shack through a break in the trees and stopped the truck. I got out, unloaded my equipment and suited up. Sitting on a split log surrounding a fire pit, I loaded my gun. It was pretty quiet around the camp area. One more peek at the map and I headed out.

I walked Spike's land for more than an hour and didn't hear or see anything. I first went east of the camp, then south, then back to the camp and up north toward a creek. Nothing. I told myself I wasn't going to waste a day, so I went west and planned on hiking until I found something.

After twenty minutes I heard the familiar "snik-snik-snik" of a gray squirrel and got into position. He ran out into the open and stopped. I slid out from behind a large oak and took aim. I pushed the gun into my shoulder, held my breath and squeezed the trigger.

Click.

I know it was loaded. A dead shell. Not good at all. I pointed the gun at the ground and got ready to try and remove the bad round.

Blam!

The buckshot fired into the earth, blowing leaves and dirt into the air. I jumped. I'd never had a shotgun shell misfire in all my years of hunting, and especially not a delayed fire like that.

I looked back at the limb. The gray was long gone as well as any other squirrels within the sound of the gun. Just great.

I checked the spent cartridge. It was dry and looked fine, just a bad round. I loaded another shell into the chamber and pointed the gun upward into the trees and fired.

Blam!

Just as expected, a nice clean shot. I loaded another round and continued into the woods. I had to walk about five minutes until I heard the stirrings of animals again. There was a mass of scurrying up ahead. I slowed my pace and saw a group of squirrels playing about, running up and down the length of a tree.

I waited until a nice sized one paused on an open branch, and just as I was about to pull the trigger, something darted in front of my view. I lowered my gun and it was gone. At least it didn't scare off the squirrels, so I prepared for another shot.

Whoosh! There it was again. Right past my field of view. I spun around to see if anything else was out there with me in the woods. Nothing. Just the clacking of the squirrels as they continued to play.

I turned back to the tree limb and brought my gun up for another shot, but it stopped part way up. I swung it back and forth to check if it got hung on a low branch. There was nothing touching it, but as hard as I tried I could not lift the gun for the shot. The harder I pulled up, the more it pressed downward.

I gave it one hard yank up and it released. I went up and over, landing on my back. The gun went off and the force rammed the butt downward into my gut. I yelled as the solid wood stock knocked all the wind out of me.

Squirrels raced off in all directions. Leaves, bark, and pieces of limbs showered down from the peppered trees, adding insult to injury. I finally sat up, brushing off the debris. And then I saw the blur again. I looked up and it darted out of view.

"Hey! Who's out there?"

I could hear the footsteps of someone running, their feet crunching through the leaves. The sound seemed to grow louder and faster, coming from all around me. It seemed to be everywhere.

"Who's out there?"

I pushed myself up and started walking when I noticed something a tree up ahead. It was the blur, but now 20 feet up and standing on a lone branch. Just as quick, it disappeared.

I turned and went another way. The rustling was now behind

me. I spun around and saw nothing. This was now beginning to freak me out.

Turning slowing, I tried to set my position in the woods. Where exactly was I now and more importantly, where was my truck? Everything began to look the same. Same trees, same hills.

Keep yourself together.

Then I noticed someone on a small ridge, motioning me. There was something familiar about him. Maybe his frame, the way he moved.

"Dad?"

I wasn't alone. I ran toward the ridge, the weight of my pack jarring my shoulders. But by the time I reached the top, he was gone.

I scanned the horizon, nothing.

No, wait! I noticed something. The roof of Spike's cabin. I ran, small limbs ripped at my face as I tore through the brush without concern. Getting out of these woods was my only thought.

I ran toward a break in the trees and fell a few feet into mud as it opened back to the road. I pushed myself up and saw my pickup, facing me, a few yards away. Panting hard as I stumbled up the road, I wiped my muddy hand against my shirt and dug into my pocket for the keys.

I coughed out a mix of phlegm and mud and buckled as a cramp dug hard into my side. *Air, just need air.* I finally made my way to the truck.

I righted myself and saw something exit the woods behind the truck. It was tall, well built, looked like a man, but he was in costume. I could swear he was wearing leather pants and boots, real old school. Some kind of colorful chest-piece and even, from this distance, a headdress.

The Chief?

He started moving toward me in a very determined fashion. I walked quickly to the driver's side of the truck, trying to feel for the ignition key with my cold wet fingers.

Key found. . . in the door. . . door opening. I tossed my pack and gun into the cab. With that he broke stride and came full speed toward me. He raised his right arm and in his hand was a large ax.

Oh no, I thought. *He's got a tomahawk!*

I jumped into the truck, slammed the door and jammed the key into the ignition. I cranked the engine and said a quick prayer as he was almost at the back of the vehicle. It started on the first try. I kissed the steering wheel and floored the pedal.

"Eat mud," I shouted as a spray shot from the back wheels before they grabbed earth and launched me forward. I did my best to traverse the ruts in the well-worn road. I hit a puddle and it showered mud up the passenger side completely covering the half open window and coating part of my arm.

I took the next turn a bit too fast, and the backend swerved off of the road and clipped a small tree. The hit jarred me so hard I lost grip of the steering wheel and it spun around like a Camden Park bumper car. I screamed as my fingers got whacked with the steering wheel crossbar. I felt fire in my hand as my right pinky now jutted out in a most unnatural angle.

There was a thump in the rear of the truck as the vehicle shifted down in the back. He was standing on the back bumper, hanging on the tailgate. There was a loud metallic clank and I looked in the mirror to see him strike the tailgate with the tomahawk, cutting right into the metal.

I growled as I grabbed the wheel the best I could, and then floored the truck again. The tires hooked into several different ruts, and we swung violently side-to-side while gaining speed. I could barely hold on to the wheel as the tires darted from worn rut to rut, but somehow he held on tight like a bull rider, one hand on the tailgate, the other swinging madly, chopping away at the truck.

The road smoothed out and became much drier, the truck picking up speed. Way too much speed for this twisting back road. But my foot was locked down hard and was not coming up.

I looked back and saw the Chief step over the shredded top of the tailgate and into the bed. Though he was aged and wrinkled, he moved quite well. The truck bumped and bucked, but the old man took slow and steady steps, riding along with the rhythm of the road.

I saw the intersection for the main road up ahead and cut hard for it. The Chief slid to the side of the bed then stopped himself with his foot on the sidewall. He pushed himself back into the middle of the truck bed.

I was now on paved road, and the truck was darn near floating, but I still couldn't shake him. At this speed, I barely had time to take my eyes off of the road to see what he was doing. When I glanced up, our eyes instantly met. He was in the back window, his aged face streaked with red and white war paint. His eyes burned like fire.

I watched helplessly as he reared back with that enormous tomahawk and braced myself for the impact. We flew past the "Welcome to Chief Cornstalk" sign. *Oh the irony, old boy,* I thought. I held the wheel for dear life, waiting for him to come smashing through. . . .

Then nothing. No smashing, no glass everywhere, no tomahawk cracking my skull in half. I glanced up, cringing as I did, and he was gone. Maybe on the roof? I listened. Nothing but the engine's roar, begging for me to let up. And so I did.

I took my foot off of the pedal. No braking, just a slow release of the gas. I could make out the trees again, they were no longer a blur. Now the only sound louder than the engine was my pounding heart.

I turned onto 2 and drove a few miles. Just enough to get my senses about me. Enough to slow the pounding in my head and clear my vision as those tractor-trailers raced by. I pulled into the lot of Timbo's, its sign proudly proclaiming, "The Coldest Beer in the State." That was a bet I was soon going to take.

I stopped the truck, opened the door and darn near fell out of the seat. My legs were jello, I was a wreck. I walked around to the back of the truck and stopped at the sight. The tailgate looked like it was butchered by a chainsaw. The holes were hacked clean through.

I noticed something in the bed of the truck. I jumped up into the back and walked across. Jammed between the bed and the rear window was a feather. It was long, not like a feather I'd seen around here before. It was his. Maybe his calling card.

I hopped out of the truck and walked across the lot to the store. Time to buy Dad a beer.

Walking the Path
Lesley Conner

Lesley Conner grew up along the Ohio River in Ravenswood, WV. In 2004, she graduated from WVU with a BA in English. Today, she lives near Hagerstown, MD, with her husband and two daughters, but dreams of a day when she can move her family back to her home state.

Monongalia County, WV
    August, 1961

    Memaw's hand was soft and warm, wrapping Susan's fingers in comfortable strength. The two stood on the cracked cement porch of Memaw and Pappy's little house, Memaw holding a basket stuffed with biscuits, strawberry freezer jam, and squares of a quilt she was going to piece with her sister that afternoon. Susan slipped her dirty feet into a pair of Keds belonging to Aunt Iris. They flapped when she walked, slapping her soles in a quiet applause, as she headed across the yard towards the narrow strip of woods separating Memaw's house from the home of her sister, Dorothy. A sliver of a path cut through the woods, allowing the sisters to come and go without driving out Summer School Road and around Nicholson Loop, which was good because neither woman had a license.

    Pride filled Susan's chest, swelling her five-year-old lungs until they felt near bursting with pleasure. She stayed with Memaw nearly every Friday night, listening to stories, playing with Aunt Iris, and soaking in the attention that came with being the only child in the house. Most Saturdays were spent in the shadows of Aunt Iris, listening to Elvis 45s, dancing the cha-cha, learning everything she could about being a teenager. Today, though, Aunt Iris had gone to the library to finish a report for school. Instead of sending Susan home, where she would be one of four children, Memaw decided to take her oldest grandchild to Dorothy's for the day.

Long blades of grass brushed against Susan's legs as the two stepped off the porch and crossed the yard, painting warm, summer sunshine on her ankles. With her head down, she let a smile of pure joy spread across her face as she absorbed as much of the silence of the moment as she could. It was special being here, with Memaw, all by herself. As she looked up, the path opened before her, a shaft of sunlight piercing the canopy of leaves and then vanishing, looking like a creature winking one enormous eye.

Susan stopped, feeling the tug on her arm as Memaw kept walking.

Aunt Iris said the woods were haunted. A man named Ray had taken a bad fall when he'd been out hunting and never left them. Before his death, he would occasionally stop by to see Pappy on his way home from work. The two would sit on the porch, drinking beer and shooting the breeze.

"He always scared me, Susie. Every time he was here. I think he liked that I was scared, because after he would jump out at me from some dark corner and yank my hair, he would laugh while I cried. Now, with him dead and all, he terrifies me." Aunt Iris had told her this one morning when they got ready to make the trip between the two houses. It was her explanation for why they ran the whole way up the steep, root-choked path. If they were fast enough, the sounds of Aunt Iris shouting for Susan to keep up and the whooshing air filling and escaping Susan's lungs might be enough to keep Ray away.

Once, at the top of the hill, Aunt Iris had turned back to face the woods. Her face was flushed and her eyes wide. Between gasping breathes she'd said, "I always thought he'd come by so often to see Mama more than to see Daddy." A rumble of laughter rolled out of the woods, sending both girls scrambling to the safety of the house.

"Come on, child. We don't have all day." Memaw's words brought Susan backed to the yard.

Fear consumed the pride and joy she'd felt a moment before, chasing the warmth radiating from Memaw's hand out of Susan's arm and leaving her fingers icy. She tilted her head upwards, looking at the firm set of her grandmother's jaw.

Memaw wouldn't run. Her steps were slow and steady, never rushing. The only reason the ghost had never gotten Susan was because she ran the entire way, pushing her legs to climb the hill between the two houses and praying she didn't trip on a tree root. If she walked with Memaw, the ghost was sure to step from the trees and eat her on the spot.

Words wouldn't form to tell Memaw she couldn't go. She shook her head, her feet firmly planted, light brown curls bouncing around her face. A sigh escaped from between Memaw's lips, sounding rough in the soft sunshine of the morning.

"Your Aunt Iris is a fool-headed teenager who has you scared of nothing but shadows. There isn't anything in those woods but the creatures God intended."

"But Ray."

Memaw's hand tightened around Susan's, no longer reassuring.

"Nothing but a story Iris has told to frighten you." Memaw took a step forward, dragging Susan closer to the shadows beneath the trees. "Don't you want to see Aunt Dorothy?"

Susan nodded. She loved going to Aunt Dorothy's house. It smelled of freshly brewed coffee, mixed with the musty scent of a parakeet cage needing cleaned. A fried bologna sandwich, made with store-bought bread, would be pushed into her hands, and she would get to spend the entire morning watching cartoons on a color TV, with the drone of Memaw and Aunt Dorothy's conversation buzzing in the kitchen.

Susan nodded again.

The two moved forward, stepping onto the path. The shadows clinging to the forest stole the warmth of the late summer sun, leaving Susan chilled. She tried to ignore the eerie silence, focusing instead on the thought of the sandwich she would soon be eating. She thought of crispy texture of the bread, the way her teeth would press it down before finally slicing through to the spongy bologna beneath. The bologna would be salty, leaving a greasy taste on her lips and fingers, lasting for hours.

After a few steps, Susan began to relax. Memaw's steps fell with the regularity of a heart beat, never speeding or slowing, but keeping a steady bum-bum that moved them farther and farther from the yard. Her face was pointed upwards, her eyes never leaving the edge of the path disappearing over the top of the hill. Susan fixed her eyes on the same spot, imagining Memaw was watching for Aunt Dorothy's yard, just as she was.

A burst of wind clapped the leaves around them together, praising her for being brave. Courage grew within Susan with each step. Memaw was right, there was nothing to be afraid of.

Except me.

The wind died down as the words slithered between the branches stretching overhead. Susan's courage died with the leaves' applause. She jerked her head skyward, looking for the speaker. Memaw's steps kept their regular beat, causing Susan to trip in her too-large shoes when her feet stopped but her arm didn't.

"You need to keep your feet under you, Susie. Your mama won't want your knees all scraped up because you were looking for something that isn't there."

Susan's face grew warm and prickly. Memaw's fingers squeezed her hand, giving her the strength to drag her line of sight back to the path and to take another step. With each step she took, Susan told herself there was nothing to be afraid of. She knew Memaw would never do anything to put her in harm's way.

I like little girls. They're tasty.

Susan jumped forward, her feet taking off in a run even though she was anchored to Memaw by her hand. Memaw held firm, not even jerking at the sound of the voice. Her stance and footsteps seemed even more solid than before, stopping Susan's attempt to flee before it began.

"It's only the wind."

Susan would've felt better if only she could see Memaw's eyes. She wanted to look deep within the calming blue and see the truth in her words, but Memaw never took her eyes from the top of the hill.

The leaves are still.

A squeak escaped Susan as she realized the voice was right. Not even one leaf was blowing in the wind, they were all perfectly still.

"Please, Memaw, please." She danced in place as she looked up at her grandmother. Hot tears burned at the back of her eyes. They needed to get out of the woods. Didn't Memaw know that?

"We'll not run. Not from nothing."

A weight settled in Susan's legs, leaving the toes of Aunt Iris's shoes dragging along the dirt path with each heavy step. Her stomach rolled, the pancakes she'd eaten for breakfast riding the wave and threatening to come lurching into her mouth.

A cold breeze swept along Susan's neck, goose pimples rising along her spine and the back of her arms. A twig snapped on the path behind her. Memaw's hand clutched Susan's, shaking her arm as her grandmother jerked at the sound, but her jaw held firm.

"It's nothing." The words sounded weak to Susan, weak and unsure. She craned her neck to look behind her. A black shadow, thin and jagged like a claw, skittered off the path and into the woods. Her hair, hanging over her shoulder, was yanked, whipping her head around. A moan leaked from between Susan's lips as pee ran warm down her legs. Looking up, she saw Memaw staring down at her, her eyes hard and her lips curled in disgust.

Present day

    The humiliation of that day came rushing back to Susan, leaving her skin hot and sticky, even though the November air was crisp and cool. She hadn't gotten her bologna sandwich or been allowed to watch cartoons. Memaw had dragged her the rest of the way to Aunt Dorothy's house and called her mom, who'd come to get her. Once they'd gotten home, her mom spanked her, saying with four kids she didn't need the extra laundry of a grown girl peeing herself. She'd been sent to bed, sore and confused.

    Shoving her hands deep into the pockets of her coat, Susan squinted at the woods, looking for any clue of the path. As Memaw and Aunt Dorothy had gotten older, no one used it, allowing the woods to take it back. Now there was only a narrow opening between the trees, carpeted with ferns and clogged with a rhododendron bush hanging with honey suckle.

    "That might be it." The words came out in a whispered cloud. Evidence that she was talking to herself. Suddenly, embarrassment took a hold of her, showing her how ridiculous it was for a grown woman to be standing by herself at the edge of the yard, looking for a ghost who'd scared her as a child.

    "It was only my imagination anyway. There's nothing out here." She turned to head back to the warmth of the house.

    Nothing, except me.

    Grinding her teeth together until her jaw jutted forward, Susan kept her footsteps slow and even as she walked back to the house. She wouldn't let stupid stories and childhood nightmares frighten her anymore.

    A baritone laugh rumbled around her, vibrating the air, raising the hair on her neck.

    You're just like your Memaw.

Here Be Demons
Karin Fuller

Like she says in this story, Karin (Tauscher) Fuller grew up in Nitro, WV, and now resides in South Charleston, WV, with her husband, Geoff, and daughter, Celeste. Karin's weekly newspaper column, which appears in the Sunday Gazette-Mail, *was named best in the U.S. by the National Society of Newspaper Columnists in 2003. She writes other stuff, too.*

October 31, 1981

It was, as we writers like to say, a dark and stormy night. The clouds were heavy, but moving fast, backlit by a nearly full moon. A Hollywood film team couldn't have assembled a more perfect setting for Halloween.

My three friends and I, all seniors that year at Nitro High, were still dressed in the costumes we'd worn to a school party. Back then, the high school was still located on 21st Street, about a half-mile from Ridenour Lake. My family lived half way between the lake and the school, and it was our house my friends and I were heading toward after the party. If it's possible to be drunk just from sugar consumption, I expect we'd have blown a .08 on the Breathalyzer. Our reckless abandon with Mountain Dew, Butterfingers, and Sour Apple Bubble Yum had us all feeling giddy, and we walked—arms linked—right up the middle of the street chanting "Lions and tigers and bears. Oh my!"

We were nearing the street's only apartment building when a car pulled up behind us and tooted its horn for us to move out of the way. Once it had passed, my friends reassembled into their linked-arm position and motioned for me to join them, but I was distracted by the house up the hill, the one behind, yet far above, the apartments. *Had I just seen a light?*

Unless you knew where to look, the house was easy to miss. It was almost completely hidden behind trees that had been smothered by kudzu, accessible only by a steep and narrow cement staircase that had broken and tilted over the years.

From the time I was small, that house had fascinated me, and I spent many hours trying to muster the courage to peek through its windows. Everyone knew it was haunted. A house like that just *had* to be haunted. Otherwise, why was it empty?

But so speaks the innocence of youth. I've now reached the age where the many stairs to that house are more frightening (and dangerous) than anything paranormal.

Then, there it was again! Another quick flash of light. Hardly more than what a lightning bug's butt would put out, but we'd already had several hard frosts. Lightning bugs, for that year, were no more.

Emboldened by the cloak of evening, I challenged my friends to sneak into that house with me and stay there until midnight.

No one spoke.

I upped the stakes, made it a double-dog dare. It would've been shameful to decline a double-dog dare. I watched as they exchanged a few nervous glances, but then, they agreed.

First, though, we stopped by my house to get flashlights, and the only cheerleader in our group ransacked my room until she found several small hand bells and a package of incense, insisting the items held powers that would ward off any demons we might encounter. Of course, the twins and I teased her for bringing those things, although I noticed that (by sheer coincidence, I'm sure) we three had found and put on cross necklaces. Great minds think alike.

I suppose I should pause for a moment to insert a few details. First of all, our cheerleader friend, a tall, gorgeous blonde, was the type of character who inspired a great many people. Mostly, she inspired them to write blonde jokes. And second, as I said earlier, we'd been to a Halloween party and were still wearing our costumes. I was dressed as the Cat in the Hat, the twins were Thing One and Thing Two, and our cheerleader friend was a ghoul (with fab taste in shoes).

Out of respect to my friends, I will keep their names private and refer to them by their costumes from this point forward.

I noticed something ominous in the air as we walked toward the house, but then—this *was* Nitro. Land o' chemical plants. A town known far and wide for its skunk-like pollution. Again, my friends and I linked arms, but now, there was no giggling and merriment. We linked to draw strength from one another.

When we reached the stairs, which were far too narrow to go four-across, they nudged me to the front. It had been my idea. That made me the leader.

Climbing so many stairs should have left us winded, but we ascended so slowly it had little effect. The door was solidly locked, the knob so frozen in place that it didn't even jiggle. Flashlights in hand, we began moving from window to window, until the cheerleader found one in the kitchen that was open.

Carefully, my friends followed me through the window. (I'm still not sure why I didn't simply crawl through alone and then open the door.) Staying close together, we explored the first floor. Instead of bones, dismembered body parts, and bloody handprints, all we found were empty boxes, food wrappers, beer cans, and cigarette butts. It was disappointingly dull.

The upstairs were next. As we climbed the curved wooden staircase, the first thing I noticed was that there were no squeaks. The steps were solid and silent. Don't *all* stairs squeak? It struck me as strange.

When I moved from the stairs to the floor, it felt spongy, gave more in places than it should. Like the stairs, there were no squeaks, and although that second floor *did* stink something awful—a rotten-egg, sulfury smell—how scary was a stinky house with quiet floors? I'd been to grade school carnival haunted houses that were creepier than this.

So my friends and I were getting pretty cocky right about then. Thing One and Thing Two kept jumping out at each other, making weird sounds or yelling "Boo!" We horsed around all the way back to the kitchen and were poking around in the cabinets there when I spotted a door with three bolts and an eyehook. There appeared to be something painted on the door, but my flashlight batteries were too weak to make out the words. I struck a match and read it out loud.

"DOWN HERE BE DEMONS."

Thing One giggled and said, "We should not be here. We should not be about."

"We should not be here when the demons are out," added Thing Two.

But our blonde cheerleader ghoul was already sliding open the bolts, and before we could stop her, she had trotted down to the basement in her cute little shoes, leaving the three of us frozen in place.

And then something went bump. *How that bump made us jump!*

I wanted to run. I wanted to flee. But what of my ghoul-friend? What if she needed me?

The Things and I huddled at the top of the stairs, illuminating the basement as best as we could with our faltering flashlights. We could hear our friend's voice, but had trouble understanding her words. Then we heard other voices. Deep, gravely voices with the rumble and vibration of an idling semi.

"We be demons," one of them said.

I heard our friend giggle.

"And I be a ghoul," said she.

After listening to several minutes of confusing blonde-speak, we heard one of them sigh deeply and send her away. A few moments later, she joined us again at the top of the stairs. We all hugged her tight.

"I can't believe you went down there!" I said. "Weren't you scared?"

"Scared?" said my blonde friend, her head tilted to the side like a confused Cocker Spaniel. "Why would I be scared? Even *I* know that demons are a ghoul's best friend."

Fleshman Cabin #6
Ellen Thompson McCloud

Ellen McCloud was born in Omaha, NB, and moved to Logan, WV, when she was six months old. She considers West Virginia her home and could not imagine living anywhere else or raising her children somewhere other than the Mountain State.

"Wake up, sleepy head. We're almost there," Luke said. The jeep moved along the partially graveled road. Candace, recovering from the unsettling dream, sipped from her water bottle and pointed at the small log structure in the distance.

"That must be it," she said. Hair prickled down the back of her neck. *Something isn't right.*

The quaint four-room cabin had looked perfect in the brochure. The location was ideal for hunting, nestled deep in the woods of Cabwaylingo State Forest. Luke pulled the ragtop Cherokee to a halt about ten yards from the cabin.

"Looks like the road ends here." Luke popped the door open. "Come on, Candy Girl, let's go check it out."

Candace grabbed her camera and led Luke up the narrow footpath.

Fall leaves blanketed the cabin grounds. The overcast sky dulled the horizon as Candace recalled images of the dream. Fragmented scenes from the dream replayed as Candace reminisced. *Don't leave me alone with these things!* she remembered saying. She watched as Luke walked away and gunshots rang out in the night. Dread overcame her, halting her steps. The memory flooded her senses, making it difficult to breathe.

"Are you all right?" Luke asked. "What's wrong?"

"I was just admiring the scenery," she answered, keeping her thoughts to herself.

"Let's go inside." Glancing up, she saw the hand-painted slat board that read *Fleshman #6*.

Candace had reserved the cabin at Luke's request. He wanted the last cabin on the state forest map surrounded by thick timber. The dense oak trees were perfect blind for squirrel hunting.

"Fleshman #6 is as deep as they come," the park ranger had said. "Lloyd will have it all fixed up for you."

They stepped onto a small stone porch, where a simple wooden weather-worn chair sat near the door.

Luke pulled the screen door open, revealing the main door standing ajar. "Looks like someone forgot to lock up."

"Maybe it was the caretaker guy getting it ready for us." Candace stepped into the cabin's living area.

The clouded sun offered little light through the windows of the cabin as they explored each room. The only door in the open cabin was on the bathroom. Candace liked the airy feeling of the place. Sparsely furnished with rustic pine chairs and a huge oak table, the hunter's cabin was minimal on amenities. No electricity, no telephone, and no television.

"Talk about off the grid." Luke walked across the mismatched colors of pine flooring in the main room.

Candace found the bedroom area and smiled. "Oh, look at this." She jumped backwards onto the bed sinking into the feather mattress. "It's so comfortable." Candace relaxed her arms over her head.

Luke sat on the edge of the down filled bedding.

"My grandmother had one of these things," Luke said. He moved beside Candace and hugged her. "Thank you, Candy Girl."

"For what?"

"Being such a great girlfriend."

***

Unpacking the jeep, Candace heard the rumbling of a vehicle traveling the rough road. Music blared from the speakers as the coarse voice of an obviously tone-deaf man sang between the backfiring of the muffler. "I keep a close watch on this heart of mine. I keep my eyes wide open all the time..."

"What on earth?" Candace watched as the old 1970-something pickup rambled into sight, splitting a mud hole and bouncing to the left of the road.

"Hey, it's Johnny Cash," Luke said, pulling a duffle bag from the back of the jeep. "Or that hillbilly caretaker dude."

"Luke! His name is Lloyd."

The truck, covered in mud, splotches of red paint, and bondo, slid to a stop.

"Hey, y'all," Lloyd yelled over the radio, his gapped-toothed grin startling Candace.

"Hello, Lloyd."

"Just checkin' on you folks. Need wood or kerosene?" Lloyd hung his arm out of the window, dirty red flannel shirt rolled up to the elbow.

"We're fine so far," Luke answered.

Lloyd eyed Luke's shotgun, which leaned up against the bumper of the jeep.

"Huntin', are you, boy?"

"Sure hope to get some squirrels." Luke smiled. "I've been planning this trip for weeks."

Lloyd spit tobacco juice out the window and wiped his chin. "We don't get many city folks up 'round here."

"I'm from Charleston." Candace pointed to Luke. "He's from Logan County."

Lloyd regarded her from head to foot. "Not many women come

to the huntin' cabins." Lloyd grinned. His gaze made Candace uncomfortable. She folded both arms over her chest. "Well, be careful, the woods can play tricks on city folks." Lloyd put the truck into gear and winked at Candace. "Bye, y'all!"

Spinning tires slung leaves and mud as he pulled back onto the road. The music started again. "Because you're mine, I walk the line."

"City folks." Luke shook his head, carrying the duffle bags and shotgun inside. "That was interesting."

"You mean disturbing." Candace followed with an armload of bags. "Oh my gosh, did you see him wink at me?"

"Probably not used to seeing pretty girls. You're hot!" Luke joked.

"Shut up." Candace frowned at him. "What did he mean by woods and tricks?"

"Nothing, Candy Girl. Let's get unpacked so we can go for a hike."

***

The multicolored leaves covered the small path and hillside. The air was crisp as it whispered through the trees. The gentle rustling of the leaves was all that broke the otherwise peaceful setting.

"It's so quiet." Candace hushed her voice as if trying not to disturb the tranquility of the forest.

Luke walked ahead, his camouflage boots crunching dried leaves and twigs. Luke knew his way around the woods.

"I started hunting with my father when I was five years old. When I wasn't hunting, I camped during the summer and explored the mountains. I love it out here."

Candace watched Luke move a few yards ahead.

"Me, too. It's prettier than I'd imagined." Candace stopped to snap a few photos. "What was that?" she said, lowering the camera.

"What? I didn't see anything." Luke motioned for Candace to

come down the embankment.

"There," she said pointing. "I saw something move."

"It was probably a squirrel. Cabwaylingo is loaded with them."

"No, it was bigger." Candace stared at the camera's viewfinder reviewing the pictures.

"Look! See, it's something else. Right there."

Luke walked back and studied the images. "It looks like a branch."

"It looks like a shoulder!" Candace showed Luke the two photos, one plainly defined the outline of a man's shoulder and side, the second showing only a shoulder.

Red flannel?

"It's as if he's hiding," Candace added.

"Who is hiding?" Luke asked.

"Lloyd." Candace said.

"Why would he be out here?"

"I don't know, Luke. You tell me."

"Could have been a hunter." Luke started to walk on.

"I want to go back," Candace said, putting the camera away. "I'm going back." The same unsettling feeling knotted her stomach as she trudged down the hill towards the cabin.

"Okay," Luke followed her. "Don't let the woods freak you out. We're as safe as kittens out here."

***

Back at the cabin, Candace continued to think about the photos while stirring the chili.

"I don't know Luke." She raised her voice so he could hear her from his spot in the living room. "It was just weird. I feel like someone was watching us." She furrowed her brow as she recalled the nightmares. "Maybe we should go home."

"Big imagination." Luke pulled the shotgun chamber open, making a loud click. Candace jumped. "You just have to get used to it, that's all. Relax, Babe."

Relax? Big Imagination? Someone was watching us and he says relax? Candace frowned. She didn't like it when Luke made light of her concerns.

"I suppose." Candace turned off the kerosene stove and joined him on the big chair. "You have to admit this is a long way from my photography studio."

"Lo-o-ng way." Luke smiled. "Let's eat, that smells great." He kissed her forehead and set the shotgun against the hearth. "I'll build a fire after we eat. Cold fall nights and fireplaces were made for each other."

The fire's flames danced within the inner hearth licking the stones and filling the room with the scent of burning pine logs. The popping and crackling of the fire, combined with the warmth, was soothing to Candace. She had all but forgotten about being frightened earlier on the hike.

She snuggled beneath the blanket. "I could get used to this."

"Well, we have three days, so enjoy it." Before Candace could reply, a loud bang startled them.

"What was that?" Candace removed the blanket and sat upright.

"Sounded like the back door." Luke grabbed his shotgun. "Stay here. I'll go check." He walked into the kitchen and Candace heard him try the door handle. "It's locked," Luke said. "Nothing out there. I looked out the window. Must have been a raccoon in the garbage. They roam at night." He rejoined Candace by the fire. "No worry, Candy Girl." He replaced the gun beside the hearth.

"Luke, are you sure?" Her fears resurfaced as she glanced around the room. "We should close the shutters."

"I will if you want me to, but we are fine. Really."

"I'd feel better if you did."

Luke stood, stretching. "All right, Babe."

Luke went throughout the cabin securing all of the windows.

"You know, there really is no reason to worry."

"You keep convincing me, Luke." The words were laced with sarcasm as she walked into the kitchen. She had been uneasy since she'd first laid eyes on the cabin. Candace thought of Luke and how much he had looked forward to this weekend. She tried to dismiss the anxiety.

"Want a cup of cocoa?" she asked.

"Yeah, sure sounds good," Luke called from the bedroom.

***

Luke's voice trailed off as he drew the last shutter in the bedroom. His eyes caught a human-like figure that moved near the timberline. He kept the shutter cracked and observed the slow-moving shape. He watched the figure move out of sight, closed the shutter and tied it tight. Taking a few deep breaths, he prepared to rejoin Candace in the main room.

***

"Hot chocolate coming up," Candace said, handing Luke his cup and sitting down opposite him. "I'll try to stop being so jumpy from now on." Candace sipped the cocoa. "I've never been in the woods before. I'm not an outdoorsy type, like you."

Luke nodded, holding his cup.

"What is it?" Candace noticed the telltale look on Luke's face. "Something wrong?" She continued to study him. They had been together for over three years, and she knew that look meant something was bothering him.

"No, I'm just tired." Luke sipped the warm cocoa and offered a slight smile.

"Are you sure?" Candace searched his face again.

"Yeah." Luke placed a hand on her knee. "Just fine."

"Let's go to bed. A good night's sleep is probably what we both need," Candace said, placing her cup on the hearth.

"All right, I'll put a few logs on the fire, you go ahead."

***

Candace was almost asleep when Luke slid out of bed and moved silently to the window.

"What are you doing?" Candace rubbed her eyes.

"Just checking," Luke paused. "I thought I saw something before, probably just an animal or shadow."

"See anything?"

"No. It's too dark."

He climbed back into bed and finally dozed off, lulled to sleep by the crackle and pine smoke of the fireplace.

Heavy footsteps dragged across the front porch and guttural moans awakened them.

"Shhh." Luke motioned to Candace. "Stay put."

She watched as he went to get the shotgun. The sounds grew louder as he approached the front window. Candace followed after Luke.

"What is it?" she whispered.

"Hush." He put a finger over his lips. Looking through the knothole in one of the shutters, his eyes widened. He took a deep breath and swallowed hard as he moved to the side allowing Candace to witness what was happening outside. Two forms moved, staggering on the front porch, three more beyond on the lawn. Human, yet not human. Lumbering around the yard, they seemed instinctively attracted to the cabin. Grunting and clawing at the screen door, one tried to make its way inside.

"Who are they?" Candace moved behind Luke.

"I don't know!" He cocked the shotgun. "Get away from the window!"

"Go away! Leave us alone!" The moaning and groaning grew louder as Candace continued to plead, "Please! Luke, make them leave us alone!"

Luke shifted to the window and opened one shutter pointing the barrel outside. Now face to face with one of the creatures the lifeless eyes stared blankly at them. A gnarled hand broke the glass and grabbed for Luke's shoulder. Jagged nails dug into his bicep as he jerked free.

"Back off!" Luke's shout caused Candace to jump back.

"Oh, no!" she screamed as the gunshot shattered more glass, blasting into the creature's face and chest, sending putrid blood and flesh spewing from its back. The smell of rotting flesh and gunpowder was sickening. They watched as the thing fell from the landing into the yard. The others continued stumbling to the porch oblivious to the fate of the first.

"What's happening?" Candace said as another pushed through the shutters, its gray hands groping. Luke pushed her back and fired another shot.

"Get away from the windows I said!" Two more shots blasted as Candace saw the shutters slam closed.

"How many of those things are out there?" Candace's voice quivered through broken words. Luke reloaded for the third time.

"None says this Mossberg Ulti-mag." As she watched him click the pump action, two more three-and-one-half inch magnum shells entered the chamber.

"Twelve gauge chamber, ten gauge bore." Luke spoke confidently to Candace about the power of the shotgun, although she could tell he was just as scared.

Luke moved to the window and peered through the knothole. "I see two stumblin' around, maybe three" he said, speaking to Candace quietly. He slid his back down the wall and sat on the floor beside her.

"It's going to be fine. You know I would never let anything happen to you."

Candace was to the point of merely shaking, thin lines of smudged mascara drawn on her cheeks by streaming tears. "What's happening, Luke? Who are they?" Candace raised a shaking hand to wipe her eyes. "I don't understand."

"Me neither, but we have to be quiet. It's too dark to see to get out of here. We have to try and hold out until daylight." Luke put an arm around her shoulders and hugged her gently to him.

Candace shivered, her mind reeled from this horrifying experience. "I've never been so scared," she confided. "This is like a really bad dream." *Just like my nightmare.*

The noise outside became unbearable. Candace covered her ears, her fears now realized and intensified. "I want to go home! We have to get out of here, Luke!"

The sounds accompanied now by the strong odor of decayed flesh and sulphur. "Make them stop!" Candace shouted, rocking back and forth. The moans were deafening to her in this state of panic.

"Let me think. Please just shut up!" Luke ran a hand through his hair. "I have to get the jeep. It's our only way out."

"Don't leave me!" She grabbed Luke's arm. "Please don't leave me alone with these things!"

"I will get the jeep, pull up around back. You jump in, and we are out of here."

"They will get you Luke! They'll get you!"

"I can make it, trust me." He stood and reloaded putting more shells in his pocket. "Just wait on me and when I pull up, get in as fast as you can, Okay?"

Candace nodded. "Okay." Her tone was uncertain, but she would do as he instructed. Luke headed out the backdoor, closing it behind him. Candace quickly turned the latch lock. Her hands trembled as she clasped them over her mouth. She watched as Luke disappeared into the uncertainty of the darkness.

Gunshots fired as she heard Luke scream, "Crazy idiots!" followed by more gunfire. The night grew quiet as Candace waited by the backdoor. Long strands of hair clung to the sides of her tear-soaked face as she anticipated the worst.

Bracing her back against the wall, she stared into the blackness, seeing no sign of Luke. *God please let him make it to the jeep.* She watched as lethargic shadows moved back and forth across the backyard.

Suddenly, she heard the jeep start. "Oh, thank God!" The jeep headlights shined on the cabin and into the eyes of Candace as she looked out the backdoor window. The jeep came to a sudden halt as mud splattered on the porch. She flung the backdoor open, ready to meet Luke. Rushing into the blinding headlights, she leapt into the passenger side of the jeep. Closing the door, she screamed in shock.

"Howdy, Candy Girl." The coarse voice growled as she stared at the gapped-toothed tobacco stained grin in disbelief.

"Lloyd! Where is Luke?" Candace put a hand on the door latch as Lloyd spun the tires to pull out.

"There's no hope for him!" Lloyd drove around the cabin, hitting one of the creatures. "Daggone zombies!"

"Go back, we can't leave Luke!"

"I'll take care of you now, Candy Girl. No way he could have made it!" Lloyd drove like a madman down the rough road. "I come back to check on you folks after I heard the news. These things are everywhere. Callin' them the undead."

"Go back, Lloyd, I want Luke!"

"Somethin' about contaminated air from one of them power plants. Rain spread it, 'cept to folks who got no rain like us, here on the mountain."

"Go back now!" Candace wasn't listening to anything Lloyd said as she grabbed the steering wheel. The jeep veered off the road, as they fought for control. It flew across the ditch and shot skywards when it hit a mound of dirt. There was a loud crunching sound as the jeep wrapped around a huge elm tree, flinging the two of them like a couple of rag dolls into the unforgiving dashboard.

***

Candace opened her eyes hearing the radio announcer talking about emergency evacuations and "hoards of the undead." A few more words from the broadcast and the radio went silent. Lloyd was slumped over the steering wheel, tobacco juice and blood trickled from the corner of his mouth and trailed down his unshaven neck.

Candace managed to force the door open to escape the confines of the wreckage. She narrowed her eyes, trying to adjust to the darkness as she made her way up the hillside to the main road. Walking away from the cabin, she tried to hurry. Limping, the pain in her leg grew more intense with every step. *You can't stop now. . . not now,* forcing herself to continue.

Looking ahead, she saw a form moving towards her. Candace stepped into a thicket of blackberry bushes lining the stretch of road, watching silently as the shadow moved closer. Squinting, she could see more clearly and knew it was Luke.

"Luke! Thank God it's you!" She hobbled back into sight as she tried to pick up the pace closing the distance between them. She threw both arms around his neck hugging him tightly.

"Lloyd said you were dead! He said they got you!" Candace cried as she felt his arms firmly encircle her waist. "I am so glad to see you!" Drawing back, she looked up to Luke.

"Thank God he was wro—"

Candace's words fell into a scream that echoed through the mountains as her eyes met those of Luke's. The once-bright green eyes were dull, cold, and lifeless.

The Sweet Song of Canaries at Midnight
Jude-Marie Green

Blue Ridge Mountains frame the hollow land. Creeks gurgle through granite hills of stone pine. A hillock of mine tailings is covered by blackberry brambles. What was, might be again, but isn't now. Jude-Marie Green writes and yearns.

My great-aunt Suzie ran this place as a boarding house back when this was a coal-mining town. Back then, in the early years of the Depression, before the Civilian Conservation Corps, before the railroad, before the Spanish War and the German War and the Japanese War siphoned all the men and all the life out of this town, back then coal mining was all this little place had.

The scars of that way of life still exist. Easy to see the shape of a mountain of tailings under a fine covering of brambles and kudzu. The front room of the boarding house has a fat cast-iron Franklin stove, aluminum chimney pipe still crawling crazy across half the ceiling to a hole in the wall that's been covered over for decades now. But we keep the stove and the chimney for authenticity. For charm. Not sure how charming the acrid whiff of ancient burnt coal is, but the soot at least has been scrubbed clean away so as not to offend guests.

My husband, Carl, thought up the idea to convert this rambling wreck into a Bed & Breakfast. "It'll be fun, Julia," he said. "Easy money from tourists looking for authenticity," he said. "Hardly no work at all."

Well, I'll give him the first two. And the hard work, neither of us minded that, much. Carl tooled around, maintaining the property: paint here and there—I have to say I love the pink trim on the window sashes, porch glider all cleaned and perfect for sitting on a warm evening, even a few outbuildings reclaimed from age and neglect.

I was surprised when he started transplanting trees into the yard, trees he'd found in the surrounding forest.

"*Dogwoods*, Julia," he said. "That's the Dogwood coal seam, we're the Dogwood Bed & Breakfast. We need some dogwoods around for authenticity."

Ah, that word. Crept up again and again while we were renovating, appeared all over our website and advertising flyers, even made it into the reviews of our B&B when the travel magazines sent supposedly undercover reporters to check us out. Amazing how popular we became in just a couple years. Such a short time. Our ghosts undoubtedly had something to do with that.

Our crowded season was summer. We laid on some help from the local university, a cook and a maid, so I wouldn't have to do everything. Devon, the cook, slept in the same room as Mary, the maid. They both wore crucifixes, so I assumed they held to some religion, but they weren't married. Not that it bothered me, though Carl turned up his nose at first. When I pointed out that this way we'd only need one room for the help, freeing up a bed for rental, he lost his compunctions against teenagerly immorality.

I dislike early mornings, but can't run a B&B from my own bed. Most mornings I'd start with the sunrise, grousing about leaving my warm sheets.

"I hate this," I said. "How did you manage it all your life?"

Carl said, "What? Didn't catch that." He didn't have my issues with early rising, but then he liked going to bed early. Early to bed, early to rise, makes a man healthy, wealthy, and wise, he frequently quoted to me. I felt pleased with my self-restraint that I never hit him when he said that before breakfast.

"Just talking to Suzie," I said. I talked to Suzie a lot. Not that she ever responded.

"Oh. Okay," Carl said.

I started my morning by rousting out the hens for the daily eggs, harvesting something fresh from the dooryard garden, cutting some flowers for the sitting room tables, a quiet hour.

Devon arrived in the kitchen before our guests did; he'd fix some coffee and set out the dishes and glasses and silver and get ready for another crazed morning breakfast service. Mary wouldn't start on cleaning the rooms until later, so in the mornings she helped me take orders and serve.

I never ceased to marvel at how a dozen rooms of people—a couple families, maybe; a handful of couples getting away from it all; the occasional single person seeking refuge—how they could raise such a ruckus, what with toilets flushing and doors slamming and feet tramping down the staircases. Still, the noise gave us all time to put on happy faces.

Every season, at least one person would sit down to breakfast looking grumpy and out of sorts. This season was Mr. Luckhert's turn, him and his wife Sophy. They both clutched onto mugs of hot coffee like drowning folk. I went over to take their order; this wouldn't be a job for Mary, she didn't know the ropes yet.

"Hope you're enjoying your stay," I started mildly. Sure enough, Mr. Luckhert had an answer for me.

"Worst night of sleep ever," he declared. "Incessant noise all night long. I demand you put us in another room tonight, or we will leave!"

Sophy nodded vigorously. "Another room," she echoed. "We must be right next to your henhouse."

"Come again?" I said. "Our henhouse is on the other side of the yard. Did some roosters crow too early under your window?" That had been known to happen. I hoped it was not the case, this time.

"Roosters? Not hardly," the man said. "Songbirds. Little tiny birds singing shrill little songs all night long. And not outside the window, either! The noise was right inside the room!"

Bless him, he looked miserable. And maybe more scared than angry. I smiled a bit in relief.

"Oh, those," I said. "What you heard were the coal miners' canaries. My great-aunt Suzie, the original owner of this house? She used to raise them for the miners, since the company was too cheap to get 'em. The miners would take a couple into the shafts with 'em every morning, and they knew, as long as the birds sang, that the air was still good."

The general level of noise in the dining room had tapered off to just embarrassed clinks of silver against plate. The folks were listening. Good! I settled into the tale.

"You only had to worry if the birds stopped singing," I continued. "That would mean bad air, methane or maybe carbon dioxide, had risen in the shafts. Then the men would hightail it back to the surface until the problem could be fixed. Those birds were lifesavers.

"Suzie lost a few birds over the years, but never did any miners lose their lives while her birds sang. Oh, they had shaft collapses like any place else; you can't have mining without death, they go together. But not from bad air.

"Not until. . . well. They closed the mine down, a few years after the Big War. Seems the miners struck a particularly rich seam of coal, but just below that was some gas. Just bad luck. They blew open a piece of wall and let that gas loose and that was all she wrote. The canaries in the mines died, the miners suffocated, and the gas rose unnoticed until it was all through our town.

"Great-Aunt Suzie said that she knew something was wrong when the birds in the house stopped singing. She soaked a couple of towels and grabbed my uncle Bobbie, her son who was just a baby back then, grabbed him up and ran up to the roof of this house. Saved their lives doing it.

"But the birds were all dead."

I stopped, hoping Mr. Luckhert and his wife would draw the conclusion. They did.

"Ghosts? I was kept up all night by the ghosts of mine canaries?" His face looked like it couldn't decide between disbelief or amusement. Finally, he cracked a smile.

I nodded. "Yessir, that's what you must have been hearing."

He started laughing in earnest, and his wife Sophy joined in. "Most B&Bs in the catalog bragged about having ghosts," he said when he could speak again, "but no one else has ghosts of singing birds! What a great schtick! You should put it on all your advertising!" He shook his head, dabbed at his eyes, and grabbed his wife's hand.

"We don't mind your *ghosts*," he continued, "but we'd sure like another bedroom without 'em, if you don't mind."

"Well sir, all the rooms have authentic haunted birdcages," I said. "Carl, my husband, found them stacked away in an outbuilding and cleaned them up, and we had enough for every room. I guess if you'd like I can take the birdcage out of the room...?" I left the question hanging delicately.

"Oh, no," Sophy said. "Now we know what it's all about, I think it's rather sweet. I don't suppose we could buy the birdcage from you?"

And we were off, trotting down the road of commerce and authenticity.

Much later, after even the fireflies had retired for the night but before my daily peace had been re-established, I sat on the porch glider and stared at the moonless dark. I wasn't surprised when Devon quietly shut the screen door behind him and joined me on the porch.

Or rather, I was a bit surprised it was Devon and not Mary; women usually have a better sense when the story isn't quite honest.

He studied me a minute, as if not quite sure what he was looking at.

"How many of those cages did you sell?" he asked me.

"Three," I said, "and I have a house full of people who will spread the word of our haunted Bed & Breakfast."

"The cages aren't wired," he said, "and I couldn't find any other wires leading into the rooms. How'd you manage the bird noises?"

Ah, so he'd been snooping. Well enough.

"I don't," I said simply.

"You're telling me the canaries really are ghosts?"

He tried a smile but it was lopsided. It occurred to me that he was maybe a little scared; then it occurred to me that maybe he'd heard the birds' singing, too. No reason for just one guest to be lucky.

"What did you hear?" I said, curious.

He sat next to me on the glider.

"It's not what I heard, it's what I saw," he said. "Well, okay. I heard the birds chirping away. But I saw. . . I saw this sweet old lady sitting at the dressing table!" He said that all in a rush.

I smiled encouragingly.

"She was brushing her hair; ivory colored hair down to her bottom. She was singing! I saw that in the mirror. I couldn't hear her, all I heard was the birds. But there she was, stroking her hair."

He took a jagged breath. "Mary likes her. That's why we're still here." He clutched his silver crucifix in his left hand. "But shouldn't we do something? Help her find the other side, like? Find rest for her eternal soul?"

"This is her home," I said simply. "But Devon. . . Think about it for a minute. All those little birds, simple little creatures, they respond to the person who loves them, feeds them, cares for them. They wouldn't be here unless she brought them, you know."

I heard the ghostly whisper of bird song and the birdcage on the porch wavered a little in the windless night. I nodded towards the bentwood rocker across from the glider, which was slowly moving in the still night. I imagined Great-Aunt Suzie smiling.

"She wouldn't mind you praying for her. She was a religious woman," I said, "but this is her home."

A Matter of Spoons
S. Clayton Rhodes

Born and raised in West Virginia, S. Clayton Rhodes's work can be found in such anthologies as STARTLING STORIES (Fall 2008 and Winter 2010), APPALACHIAN WINTER HAUNTINGS and Apex's upcoming THE BLACKNESS WITHIN. He currently resides in Marietta, OH, with his wife and children. Visit his website at www.sclaytonrhodes.com.

The other guys were already waiting on Zack when he arrived—Roy, Carlin, Dale, and of course Kevin, glorious leader, exalted trailblazer.

Roy sprawled on the grass, toying with a length of clover stem. Carlin checked his watch, while the others whacked sticks against the hurricane fencing surrounding the complex or kicked at gravel.

They were in front of KPI, which once upon a time stood for Krupps Polymer, Inc.—a booming business until the day a busted relief valve was replaced on a certain chemical tank. Unfortunately, the new valve didn't bleed the air any better than the old one, and the tank ultimately blew like a shaken soda can, catching twenty-one men on the production line with hunks of metal like so much shrapnel. And, oh boy, did OSHA have a field day afterwards. KPI's doors closed for good some five years back.

"So what're we doing here exactly?" Zack asked.

"We're gonna play a little game," Kevin told him.

"What kinda game?"

"Spoons."

"Isn't that a kid's game?" Dale said.

"Usually. But not the way we'll play."

"And how would *our* way be different?" Zack asked.

"Trust me. It will be."

***

"You all know the rules, right? One person's 'it.' That person gets a five-minute lead. He'll find a hiding spot and lay low. The rest will enter and the search'll be on. When you find the guy who's it, keep him company 'til the others come and find you. We'll just keep going until the last guy makes it."

Normally, the idea would've sounded lame to Zack. What made things interesting was the fact the place was supposed to be haunted. A reputation followed when that many people bought the farm all in one day. The way the story went, the spirits of those men were supposed to still roam the factory. It was easy to imagine lumbering specters of The Lost Twenty-One, sporting bits of tank shrapnel from their blistered—and now rotting—husks. Moaning. Shuffling. The stuff of local legends.

Dale chewed at his lower lip. "I don't know 'bout this. I mean, what if we're caught? They got no trespassing signs all over the place."

Kevin nodded. "Nobody's twisting your arm, Dale. You wanna go home and play Barbies with your sister, that's fine by us."

That brought snickers from everyone except Dale. "Well, I'm just mentioning it, is all. We get busted, it won't be my fault."

"Yeah, sure," Kevin said. "So everyone *else* ready?"

He led the way to a waist-high rent in the galvanized fence links. Kevin had to have been here before to know about the opening, Zack realized.

Kevin thought of a number between one and twenty and asked everyone to choose a number. Carlin picked closest and Kevin pronounced him the winner.

"Carlin, lucky man, you get the prize. Get to hiding and we'll see you in a few. High tail it, now. Clock's a tickin'."

Carlin gave a begrudging sneer but ducked through the fence. "Hey, how do I get in, anyway?"

"Around the corner there's a broken-out window. I left an orange crate you can use to hoist yourself up. Oh, and we might need these . . ." Kevin stooped to pick up the sack at his feet and withdrew a blue plastic flashlight. He shook it, making the batteries inside rattle. "Got enough to go around in case anyone decides to brave the darker bowels of this place."

He smiled while passing out the flashlights.

***

After Carlin disappeared, they counted down the minutes. Then they took the same route, found the orange crate he'd used, and climbed in.

Knowing the place was off limits, knowing the chewing-out—or worse—they'd get if they were caught only made it more exciting for Zack. He took in the area they'd entered. The room held nothing but dust and stale air now, and the sound the carpet of leaves made reminded him of Rice Krispies crumbling underfoot.

From out of nowhere came a sensation like a centipede jaunting up Zack's spine.

Kevin, noticing Zack's sudden twitch, said, "What's the problem, Huddleston?"

"Dunno. I just got this feeling . . ." was all he could think to say.

"Yeah? You're not gonna start pissing in your Huggies like Carlin, are you?"

"No. Just a bad feeling."

Kevin slapped Zack's back. "Yeah, well good luck figuring *that* out. Meanwhile, let's keep looking."

Zack had to admit he was a little jealous of Kevin. Jerk though he sometimes might be, he had the kind of charisma Zack lacked. And no one gave Kevin any lip, either. Zack doubted if *his* dad ever pulled any of that you-hafta-find-your-purpose crap on him. His own dad was always saying that sort of stuff: "You hafta find your purpose, son. You hafta find your purpose."

You just knew Kevin would find a way out of this single stoplight town come graduation. Meanwhile, Zack struggled to get passing grades—another sore spot at home since it wasn't likely he'd make the cut on any scholarships any time soon. Like his old man, a future of plant work in one of the many factories still operational loomed on the horizon.

"This place is huge," Dale said. "It'll take forever."

"That's why we need to split up. Zack, why don't you and Dale search the offices? Roy and I can take the lower level."

***

Dale left Zack to check out the other side of the building. Many of the vacant offices didn't have windows and what dim light there was filtered down from the dust-caked skylights in the hallway. Zack went from room to room, searching for Carlin. It was a stupid game, really. Spoons. Any initial excitement of exploring a forbidden place was quickly wearing away.

He looked beneath work counters in what were once the research labs and opened closets. The far-off noises of Dale conducting his own searching reached him in faint echoes . . . a scuffle along floors, and the opening of his own doors.

Zack was about to move on when the same skittering centipede-up-the-spine sensation came over him again.

What the heck? he thought.

It had grown quieter, which could mean a couple of them had already found Carlin and were holing up with him. The weight of the flashlight in his back pocket reminded him there was still the lower level—the "darker bowels," as Kevin put it—to check out.

Zack found and pushed at the fire door leading into one of the stairwells. The hinges protested a bit; they hadn't seen this much use in years. It was dark within; even the dim light from the hallway didn't make it in here.

"Guys?"

No answer.

A flick of the flashlight threw a weak oval glow onto one inner wall.

Then he heard two things: an almost girlish scream (which ended all-too abruptly) and stifled laughter.

For the third time, Zack's spine became a playground for squirming, long-legged bugs to race up and down between his flesh and sweat-soaked shirt.

He shook it off. The laughter was the giveaway. The scream had been faked and one of the guys was trying unsuccessfully to keep quiet. They were down there, all right.

***

At the bottom of the stairwell, Zack turned his flashlight about, letting the beam fall on rusting machinery, bare cinderblock, and a recess in the floor where concrete steps led to an even deeper level.

It smelled worse than raw sewage down here, and the only sound besides his footsteps was the furtive rustling from below.

He smiled. Yeah, sure. That's where they were.

He didn't go down since they probably planned to jump out and try and scare the bejesus out of him. Instead, he leaned against the safety rail and trained the flashlight directly into the landing below.

And what Zack saw gave him a rush of adrenaline like ice water flushing through his veins. At first he wasn't sure what he was looking at; he only knew it wasn't good. Something roughly the size and shape of a leaf pile slunk forward at the bottom of the runoff channel on the lower level; a living mass, whose mucous-slick flesh rose and fell in slow rhythms. Zack was in time to see a leg of jeans ending in a tennis shoe disappearing beneath the thing in a wet slurp.

"So I see you found my little pet."

The sudden voice startled Zack so badly, when he turned, a handrail strut knocked the flashlight from his hand and sent it spinning into the black pit below.

Kevin stepped forward holding his own flashlight beneath his chin, making his face look distinctly ghoulish. "Booga-booga!" He laughed. "Who were you expecting, Huddleston? One of The Lost Twenty-One?"

Zack's mind raced. Had Kevin gone around the bend? He sure was talking crazy enough. What was that he said about his pet?

"You . . . know about that thing down there?"

"Who, him?" Kevin nodded toward the pit. "El sluggo? I call him Jerry. Like from Tom and Jerry, you know? Cute, huh? Oh, I get it. You want to know what he is, where he came from." Kevin took a deep sigh while coming a step closer. "Can't help you there, amigo."

"But you must have some idea." Zack edged back from the railing and further from Kevin.

"Oh, sure. I got plenty of theories. Mostly, I think of Jerry as the product of hopped up evolution."

"Hopped up . . ."

"Evolution. Yeah. Survival of the fittest. Natural selection on crack. You remember your biology, right? You know I heard of this one factory in Arkansas, probably a lot like this one, started dumping waste product into the river—before all the regulations, I guess. Anyway, this fisherman is out in his boat one day and lands a bass. With three eyes." He laughed again, making Zack think once more Kevin's brain might have turned to mush. He didn't like where this conversation was going.

"Is it really hard to believe," Kevin continued, "that something like Jerry could evolve? The way I see it, they used all kindsa chemicals in this place . . . polymers and plastics, acids and stuff. Who knows what was in that tank that blew way back when? Maybe it fused some of those guys' burnt skin together. Gross, I know, but it could've happened that way, maybe. Jerry was about the size of a football when I found him a couple years back. I fed him cockroaches and mice until he got bigger. Then he graduated to stray cats. He's pretty much helpless on his own. More harmless than a ton of Jell-O."

Zack's mind struggled to get some sort of handle on all this and failed. "But one of the guys . . . I think that thing . . ."

"Oh, yeah. That was Dale. Carlin and Roy went first. See, Carlin and I had it worked out ahead of time. He'd come down here and wait for the rest of you. I told him I'd leave a zombie mask down here for him to put on and jump out and make like he was one of the Lost Twenty-One to scare everybody."

"But there wasn't any mask."

"No. And now there isn't any Carlin." Kevin sucked at his teeth. "I took Roy out in the stairwell, then went down and got Carlin. Don't worry, though. It was quick for both of them."

"You killed them."

Kevin held up his hands in a gesture of helplessness. "Zack, what can I do? Jerry's a growing boy. The idea of luring everyone down here wasn't bad. Jerry comes up with a good one every now and then."

"It was *Jerry's* idea?"

"Sure. Oh, he doesn't say much, but we have a connection." Kevin tapped his temple. "Up here. Kind of a psychic thing going on, I guess you'd say. Didn't you feel something when you came into the building?"

Zack did, indeed. The crawling sensation up his vertebrae. He felt it now.

"How could you do it, though?" Zack shook his head. "Roy, Dale, and Carlin. How could you feed friends to that *thing*?"

"Jerry. His name is *Jerry*," Kevin insisted. "And I couldn't help it. I've spent so much time with him, he's got this hold on me now. You wouldn't understand."

It sounded like the oldest cop-out in the world to Zack. *The devil made me do it.* Still . . . the tingling coming from Jerry was growing stronger by the second. It was like a tuning fork coursing through his marrow and setting his teeth on edge.

"And now . . ." Kevin said, ". . . it's your turn." He revealed a hammer he'd been holding out of sight at his side and swung it in a flashing arc toward Zack's skull.

Zack threw an arm up to block the blow a mere second before his brains were bashed out of his head. He felt his ulna splinter and cried out at the white-hot pain racing all the way up to his shoulder.

Then Zack's feet were swept out from under him and he went down. He slid on his back, using his feet to push himself on the cold concrete, trying to get away the best he could. No way to crabwalk with only the one good arm.

His breath came short and raw, and his face pulsed with heat.

The hammer came down for another go, but instead of trying to block it this time, Zack went straight for, and caught, Kevin's wrist. It only took an easy jerk to bring him off balance. A quick foot planted in Kevin's gut, and Zack flipped him up and over and into the pit below.

Zack hadn't noticed he'd come so close to the edge. Once he got up, he steadied himself against the railing.

At the bottom of the steps, Kevin lay with his head bent at a crooked angle and his wide eyes staring vacantly at his own pooling blood. The flashlight near Kevin's head shone on Jerry. Tumorous and greasy as an oil slick, he advanced at a snail's pace. Apparently, when it came to food, Jerry wasn't prejudiced.

The message, MORE. BRING MORE . . . thrust itself into Zack's mind like an ice pick.

Yeah, sure, he found himself thinking. *No problem.*

He was curious about what would happen if Jerry continued eating. *Will you explode or just keep getting bigger and bigger?* he wondered.

WAIT AND SEE . . . was the response.

Finally, Zack's dad's hopes were going to come true. Zack had finally found a purpose. Who knew, maybe he could even talk Dad into a game of Spoons.

Shy One Pearl
Robert W. Walker

Award-winning author, Robert W. Walker has been a citizen of Charleston, WV, five years and lives with his wife and four stepchildren in the Capitol City. Rob created his highly acclaimed INSTINCT and EDGE SERIES between 1982 and 2005. He has since written his award-winning historical series featuring Inspector Alastair Ransom with CITY FOR RANSOM (2006), SHADOWS IN THE WHITE CITY (2007), and CITY OF THE ABSENT (2008). Rob's current work is DEAD ON and a three-part historical thriller ebook entitled CHILDREN OF SALEM. You can find Rob at www.RobertWalkerbooks.com.

Quarrelsome was the single word most people leveled at Detective Lucas Stonecoat, a full-blood Texas Cherokee Indian cop in Houston, and a man who proved that a Native American Indian could kick the stereotype, get off the reservation, and make a living as a police in the white world—and still keep his identity. There was much to admire about the man besides his Jimmy Smits good looks, his 6'4" lean frame, and his mesmerizing eyes. Still, he was surly and contentious ever since Pearl Sanchez had disappeared.

He kicked out at his desk, the sound sending a shot through the old police station slated for demolition.

"You gonna bring the house down before the wrecking ball?" asked Dr. Meredyth Sanger, police shrink, to whom Lucas always went for profiling help. He'd asked her for any insights she might have about the kind of man who could abduct a fourteen-year-old girl and then send little bloody pieces of her home to the family, making it clear he was chopping Pearl up little by little.

Lucas had gone over everything ten, eleven, twelve times. Everyone who worked for the father, everyone the mother had ever known, completely turning their private lives inside out in search of anyone anywhere at any time that either of the two might have crossed. Whoever was behind this crime seemed to take great, abiding joy in the suffering of Pearl's parents, Pearl being their only daughter. It stood to reason it'd be a disgruntled employee, after Al Sanchez ran a business both high powered and involving hundreds of employees. Countless employees and come and gone, many of them upset with Sanchez. None of these panned out. But each had to be checked. Meanwhile the clock ticked on for Pearl.

He'd turned then in earnest to the mother, and he found things in her past she pleaded he keep just between them, things that even Sanchez didn't know. Again none of the leads here panned out. He went back to Sanchez, tossing out the idea it was work-related, digging into his background. Could it be someone he'd crossed as a child, as a teen, as a young man in college? Nothing.

So much time wasted and nothing. The strike force had no better luck. The clock ticked on. Time was not on Pearl's side.

They finally had to cede to the notion the maniac who had Pearl was a total psycho with an agenda he alone could possibly understand. A mad agenda that had no connection to the real world. This meant no real world sensible means of looking for a motive, and without a motive—if he had simply stalked her and lifted her off the street for no reason other than to chop her up and send her piece by piece home—how could they possibly catch the fiend?

He'd remained faceless all this time.

He left no clue, as corporeal as fog, a phantom within the fog, a fog that had kept Lucas in the dark all this time. Too long . . . another digit arrived in a tidy box.

The parents recognized the knuckle and nail.

Who knew if the crazed fiend might simply next take her leg, an arm, her head, or Pearl's spleen, her heart, her stomach?

In the middle of it all, Lucas's Chief, Aaron Phillips, recently having taken over the stationhouse that'd soon be leveled, got in Lucas's face and ordered him in no uncertain terms to see a shrink other than his chum, Meredyth.

"For kicking a desk?"

"Just do it before this case overwhelms you!"

"See a shrink when the case is ongoing!" Lucas demanded.

"That's an order! No excuses!"

"But time's of the essence, Chief! We need to keep on the case, else Pearl—"

"Case'll be waiting, Lucas. This one's going nowhere."

"Nowhere?"

"Nowhere."

It was too true. In every sense of the word, the Pearl Sanchez case was going nowhere.

As soon as Chief Phillips turned his back, Lucas felt an attack coming on, one of his blackouts from a lingering condition from years past that only Meredyth Sanger knew of. He'd learned to trust her for this reason, but now she's handing me off to some shrink I don't even know? And what gives with Chief Phillips, stopping me from doing my job in the middle of my investigation? That just isn't done!

Then the blackout was over as quickly as it threatened to drop him to his knees, and he saw it . . . saw it clearly. Something had changed in Pearl's life. Her routine disrupted.

The new piano teacher.

How many times had he seen it in the paperwork. How many times had he ignored it?

Pearl was locked away in her piano teacher's basement or attic or crawl space. Little Pearl'd been taking lessons for three years, and she played at the school pageant, a regular prodigy. The pictures depicted a beautiful young Hispanic girl. But her piano teacher had died in a car accident, and she'd begun to go to a new piano teacher. It was a detail no one, including Lucas, had paid any attention to.

Lucas raced from the old stationhouse in mid-town Houston. He drove across the city with his strobe light flashing, horn blaring. He called for backup as he did so. The last package sent to her parents had held Pearl's bloody left ear. The maniac could tire of the game at any time.

"Anatomy is destiny," Sigmund Freud had said. This was a twisted truism here. At what point would the piano teacher-turned-killer decide to take a piece of Pearl that would be fatal?

He found the address that'd been in their files all along, the same address he'd subconsciously memorized. The piano teacher had been pleasant and had answered all the questions previous detectives working under Lucas had asked of her. Her alibi established, she'd claimed not to have seen Pearl for a week, not since her last session at the keys. Another dead end, so he'd thought.

So everyone had thought.

Now he stood pounding on the door. He had no warrant, so he must talk his way in, sift about the place, make small talk, find a reason to open the door to the basement, try to get a rise out of her. He calmly did it all, and Mrs. Louise Bohnheim came at him with a knife as soon as he went for the door. As soon as she attacked, Lucas put her down with a right hook and tore the door open. He took the rickety stairwell two and three steps at a time, and sure enough here was Pearl, her eyes wide, her mouth moving below the gag, her bare body shivering and covered with small cuts where the mad woman had been at play.

Lucas tore away her bonds and gag, and he lifted her into his arms, and she said thank you repeatedly in a mantra of gratitude, and he told her to save her energy, and that he'd get her to a hospital, and that she'd soon be in the arms of mother and father. Safe.

"Is that the way you remember it, Detective Stonecoat?" asked Dr. Kari Martin, the police shrink he didn't trust, despite kind things Meredyth had said about Martin.

"You can be sure she's the best, Lucas. I would only find the best for you. I love you, remember?"

"Remember?" he looked up to see not Meredyth but Dr. Martin instead. "Hold on. Whataya mean, how I remember it. That's how it was, just like I told you."

"You spoke to Pearl when you found her?"

"Yes."

"And she spoke back?"

"Yes."

"Thanked you repeatedly, you say?"

"Repeatedly."

"And when you got her to the hospital, she. . . Her eyes were open and she was conscious?"

"Yes! How many times I gotta say it?"

"Until you get it right."

"Right?"

"Meredyth said to keep at you until you get straight with this Pearl Sanchez business, detective."

"Get straight?"

"Detective, the coroner has time of death for Pearl Sanchez at twenty-four hours before you reached her."

He shook his head firmly . . . then more firmly. "That's not how it happened."

"No . . . not in your head, obviously."

Lucas swallowed hard and stared at his griddle-sized hands; they seemed far away, as if his arms were turned to rubber and stretching away from him. Martin finally broke the silence. "Detective, how long since the Sanchez case was closed?"

"Active yesterday, closed today."

"Try six months ago, Lucas."

"Six months?" Lucas looked around the office and past the office to the green walls of the institution. "Six months?"

"That's how long you've been with us here."

Doctor and cop stared across at one another in a silence of infinite depth.

"You saying, I was committed?"

"Yes."

"And Pearl Sanchez is dead?"

"Yes."

"I carried her to the hospital in my arms. Gave her to the ER people."

"Dead, sir. You carried her in dead."

"I did?"

"I'm sorry, but at least for you, this is a good day."

"A good day?"

"A breakthrough. You're aware of your surroundings."

"Pearl didn't make it?"

"You had a break down, Lucas."

"But she talked to me."

"Perhaps on some level she did; perhaps you soothed her spirit, Lucas, but her body was gone when you arrived ahhh . . . too late."

"Too late. But for six months now, playing it over and over in my mind. . ."

"You saved Pearl. You weren't too late."

"I let her down in the real world."

"It's a burden to be sure, detective, but one that we're here to help you accept."

"Accept?"

"The only way to free you."

"Free me from this place?"

"No . . . from . . . from this version of events. . ."

"Gotta accept the truth."

"Then we can talk about your going out the door."

Lucas heard faint music playing somewhere the other side of the door. He stood, pushed his chair away, and went toward the door. "I could've sworn I'd gotten there in time."

"I'm sorry. Everyone is."

"I never suspected the piano teacher."

"No one did."

"No one did in time."

Quarrelsome was the single word most people used for Detective Lucas Stonecoat, surly and contentious ever since the Sanchez case. Before that he'd been a likeable fellow, and he'd had a chance with Dr. Sanger. Not anymore. That Sanchez girl...what was her name? Pearl, a shy one, yeah . . . . He'd gotten there shy maybe twenty, twenty-four hours . . . had failed to break it in time. Now shy Pearl haunted him.

Now his badge weighed heavy.

Nigh
Eric Fritzius

Eric Fritzius relocated to WV to see his wife through medical school, but fell in love with the state and decided to stay. He lives in Mercer County where he is a freelance writer of articles, stories, and plays. A former president of West Virginia Writers, Inc., he now serves as its Webmaster and podcast host.

Helen St. John, *Starbucks* employee #73451, looked on as her de facto training-supervisor, Ted (#42752), expertly mixed a house blend double latte, slipped a cardboard-cozy onto the cup and slid it across the counter to a man holding a yellow picket sign.

"Still look like tomorrow?" Ted asked, while ringing up the order.

The man with the sign absently looked up at the boy and said, "Yes. Definitely tomorrow."

Helen thought the man was in his late fifties, though it was difficult to tell through the thick salt & pepper beard and long stringy dark hair. His clothing was quite ragged, but he didn't smell too bad.

"I'll keep a cup warm for you just in case it doesn't," Ted said with a wry smile.

The man with the sign nodded, accepted his change from Ted, then took his coffee and began moving toward the front door.

"You getting the hang of all this, so far?" Ted asked Helen.

"I think so. It's not too hard," she said. "Who was that guy, anyway?"

"That's Mr. Daniels—one of our regulars. He's been in for his double latte every morning since we opened three years ago. And I heard he came in the old diner that used to be here for years before that. Every single day. He's kind of a local fixture, I guess."

"Does he always carry that sign?"

"Oh, *'The End is Nigh!'* Spooky, huh? He thinks the world's going to end tomorrow."

"The way things are going these days, who could argue with him?"

Ted laughed. "Well, the thing is, Mr. Daniels thinks the world will end tomorrow *every day*."

"Every day?"

"Yep."

"He comes in every day and says the world will end tomorrow?"

"That's about the size of it."

"Well, that's original, I guess. And here I thought he was just some crazy homeless guy."

"No. I think he has a home. This is just what he does."

"Walking up and down the sidewalk, predicting the world will end tomorrow?" Helen asked.

"Pretty much. They say he used to teach religion at some Ivy League school up north, but got fired. He supposedly taught here at WVU for a while, but gave it up to pace the sidewalks full time. . . . And that was like, twenty years ago, or something."

Helen shook her head. "Well, I don't know what theology he's into, but he needs to reread his Bible. Remember back at the Millennium when all the TV preachers were predicting the end? I used to worry a lot about that kind of thing. Well my daddy's a Baptist minister and he told me to just remember *Mark 13:32.* . . . "No one knows about that day or hour, not even the angels in heaven, nor the Son, but only the Father." That verse made me feel a lot better. And it's true. Mr. Daniels can predict all he wants, but only God knows when the end's truly going to come. It's not coming a day sooner or later than *He* wants it to."

"Uh, yeah. Whatever," Ted said, a little suspiciously. "Um, did I show you how to work the milk jet yet?"

From outside, there came a sudden screech of tires followed by a thunk. Helen looked up in time to see a paper cup strike the front window, spraying milky brown coffee across it.

"Somebody call 9-1-1!" a lady near the window shouted, and Ted immediately snatched up the nearest phone and began dialing. Helen, however, found herself moving toward the front of the store. Beyond the brown wash on the window, she could see a shiny black luxury car—an Infiniti, she thought—parked halfway on the sidewalk. The front of its hood was dented. Helen reached the front door and knew what she would find when she opened it.

Lying in front of the car was Mr. Daniels. He was bleeding heavily from the side of his head, and some of his blood had spattered onto the yellow picket sign. He looked up with tear-filled eyes as Helen knelt down beside him. His breathing was labored, but he was still trying to speak. Helen had to lean close to hear his whispers.

"Tomorrow," he said. "Maybe the day after. . ." With that said, his breathing stopped.

"Help! Does anyone know CPR?" Helen screamed at the bystanders around them. No one responded, but she continued to scream until she heard the sound of the Infiniti's driver-side door opening. Climbing out of the vehicle was a young man with long, pale blond hair. He was very tall and wore a suit made of snow-white cloth. He was the most beautiful creature she had ever seen. When his gaze fell upon her, though, Helen felt as though she was suddenly at the bottom of a cold, dark lake. She was terrified and exalted, but somehow found her voice.

"Why?" she asked, uncertain as to what exactly she meant by it. For what seemed a long time, the young man simply stared at her with those piercing eyes, the color and depth of starlight.

"Just business," the driver said.

An ambulance soon arrived to collect Mr. Daniels's body, but no one else seemed to notice that the tall young man and his Infiniti were gone, nor that they had been there at all. Witnesses described the hit-and-run culprit to police as an old woman driving a beige Buick Skylark.

Only Helen knew otherwise, but no one thought to ask her. In fact, no one—not even Ted—seemed aware that she had not returned to work. Helen remained on the sidewalk, cradling the stained yellow picket sign in her lap.

"The End is Nigh," it read.

Helen St. John had the strangest feeling she would soon be needing it. If not tomorrow, then perhaps the day after.

Jackson Gainer's Ghost
Ellen Bolt

Born in West Virginia before television, video games, and Internet robbed us of precious hours with family, Ellen Bolt inherited countless yarns from parents, grandparents, aunts, and uncles. She now delights in sharing the tales given to her around the wood stove and in the light of an oil lamp.

Jackson never paid much mind to talk of ghosts and such like. Truth be told, he refused to have much trust in folks who sat around yammering about that sort of foolishness. This unnaturally warm October Sunday evening, however, he had nothing else to do. So he sat there in his usual place on the upturned crate at the far end of the porch of Clauson's Feed and Grain Store and listened to Howard and Lonnie swear they had witnessed a spook.

Griff sent a stream of tobacco juice across the railing and shook his head. "Lonnie, you may've seen a leaf blow by or a bird or a shadow. But no way you saw his ghost."

Clark and Taylor chuckled their agreement.

"Probably saw your own shadow," Taylor snickered. "Wouldn't be the first time it freaked you out, now would it?"

Lonnie lowered his head. "I was just a kid then."

"A kid!" Clark mocked. "Lord, Lonnie, we wuz sixteen and hauling timber for ol' Man Hayney."

"Yeah, but you gotta admit that you guys were spooked, too. At first."

Griff, noticing the red splotches on Lonnie's neck. "Lonnie's right, boys. That night when we saw that thing float up out of Maudie

Houchins's bedroom window, he wasn't the only one pickin' 'em up and layin' 'em down back to the road."

"Maybe so, but he's the only one that rounded the turn and fainted when he seen his own shadow on the clay bank." Taylor leaned back against the wall, slapped his thigh, and laughed.

Jackson had tired of hearing the telling and retelling of the story of how Maudie Houchins's ghost had appeared just as the five boys were sneaking up to her house. More than once he had started to tell 'em what they saw was just a lace curtain being snatched out the window by the wind. He wanted to tell how he had watched from that very window as they scrambled across the moonlit field. But each time he started to tell, feelings of guilt, shame, and anger crept over him and he held his tongue.

Like always they started rehashing their experience. Griff figured the "ghost" was just shadows made by moonlight filtering through the big oak. While some agreed and others argued, Jackson's memory wandered back to Maudie's house that late autumn night fourteen years ago.

He recalled helping his ma put the house in order just like she promised Maudie they would. They swept and folded and put away. They wiped up every speck of dust, even from under the bed and around the pictures, the mantle clock, and the big mirror over the dresser. They opened windows to air out the place. Jackson remembered grumbling that since the old woman was dead, it didn't matter if the house wasn't perfect when her snooty sister came to claim it.

He remembered the hardness in his ma's eyes when she reminded him that Missus Houchins had paid them—had paid them well—just two days before and added that when you give your word, it's a contract every bit as binding as a written agreement. And their contract with Missus Houchins hadn't got cancelled by the Death Angel.

It was a fact that Maudie had paid them extra good. It had been hard for her to talk with the coughing and wheezing. But that day when they took her potato soup and bread, she motioned for Ma to leave it on the bedside table. Then she whispered his name.

"Jackson. Come here, boy. Come here."

Even now the memory of how she peered up through those gray, sunken eyes chilled him. He had inched a step closer and felt his ma's hand nudge him right up to the bed. Just remembering made him shiver.

"Jackson, you been good to me. Not like them others. You helped when I asked you to fetch wood or gather apples. You cleared snow off'n the porch and down to the mailbox. And you always kept a civil tongue in your head."

The words echoed so clearly through his memory that Jackson almost turned to look for her now.

"You're a good boy, Jackson. We both know that I never paid a piddlin' dime for your work."

He remembered the lump in his throat as he tried to protest. He remembered how the sick old woman looked like she had heard him grumble to his ma about never getting paid for the work. He could still hear the weak, raspy cough and see her sinking back into the dingy pillow, tears squeezed from her closed eyes. He was sure she was gone, but after a couple of shallow breaths, she had pointed a bony finger toward the dresser.

"Look in the middle drawer, boy. There's a tobacco poke..." She coughed and waited to go on. "... tobacco poke. Get it."

Ma had nodded for him to do it, so he pulled out the drawer and looked down at a tangle of bloomers and stockings.

"Left corner."

He could still feel his hand moving reluctantly under the dying woman's personal stuff until he touched the pouch. It was hard, heavy.

She smiled as he lifted the pouch from the drawer. At least he thought she smiled. Maybe it was pain pulling at her face.

"That's yours, boy. Ol' Maudie wants you to have that. All of it." She had stared up at the ceiling while she caught her breath again. "Don't want my uppity sister to have one—" She coughed again. "—red cent."

Jackson tried to remember if he had even thanked her. Probably, since his ma was there to nudge him. He remembered well what happened next though.

The scrawny old woman tried to roll onto her side.

"Help me, Ester," she pleaded to his ma. "Boy, reach under—" She let her arm drop behind her as his ma lifted her to her side.

"Under mattress. See it?"

Jackson closed his eyes, leaned across the railing to face the breeze. Fourteen years later he could still smell the must and urine odor of that bed. But he had done as he was told and reached under the mattress. He moved his hand until he felt a lump. He watched the color drain from his ma's face as she unwrapped the faded rag he had handed her. They looked down at a stack of bills.

"Yours, Ester. Yes, you take it. Won't do me no good—" She coughed again. "—where I'm goin'. 'Sides, I owe you and your boy."

Eight hundred and ninety-four dollars. The most money he had seen in one stack before or since. He remembered thinking that his pa could stay drunk for months on that. But that was not to be.

They had left Maudie Houchins there in the stinky bed and went home without speaking of their windfall. The next day when his ma went back with more warm food, Missus Houchins hadn't opened her eyes or said a word. The next day she was dead, and they cleaned her house. Still they didn't talk about the money, and he was pretty sure his ma hadn't told his pa, for he kept grumping about how hard he had to work to make ends meet. That meant "to buy a bottle."

Jackson never knew where or how his pa scraped together enough to buy the whiskey he drank while he and his ma cleaned Maudie's house. He just knew that the old man tramped out of the kitchen muttering and wasn't back when they got home. Ma figured he had gone snooping around the Houchins place looking for the still Maudie had busted up after the doctor told her she had the cancer. Jackson recollected the tiredness in his ma's voice when she told him to go back there and make sure they had closed all the windows and "look for the old bastard."

Many a time Jackson had relived that night in Maudie Houchins' house. He had not taken a light since the full hunter's moon bathed their world with a dream-like glow when he set out through the pine grove. He'd only be gone half an hour. But inside he found his pa sprawled across Maudie's bed, whimpering and muttering about what a good old woman she had been and what good moonshine she had brewed. Jackson recalled how he had tried to get the drunk to his feet, but the man's wobbly legs doubled under him and they both fell. Jackson could still feel the warm, slick vomit on his hand, and the smell still turned his stomach all these years later.

He remembered the voices of Griff and the others as they came laughing across the field. They'd come to search for the still, too, he guessed. He'd rose to his feet, dreading to have them find him and his pa here. Then the wind had sucked the curtain out the window sending them scattering like a flock of scared geese.

Jackson grinned, thinking of his friends running from a dingy lace curtain, but the grin soon faded when he remembered dragging his pa to a chair and getting a pan of water and the jug of Fleecy White his ma had set on the kitchen shelf. He closed his eyes, attempting to shut out the image of himself down on his knees trying to clean up the puke and hearing the splash behind him. The old man had tottered to his feet, peeing against the wall.

He could never clearly remember what followed. Maybe he hit his pa with something—the jug of Fleecy White, maybe. Or maybe he just shoved him. Anyway, the old man went down and hit his head on the dresser. Jackson did remember thinking that he couldn't clean up another mess. He had gone to the kitchen and took Maudie's matches from the cabinet. He'd seen her put them there the day she had him burn a brush pile. Then he remembered sitting in the pine grove and watching sparks dance up into the night sky. His ma came and sat beside him with her arm around his shoulder.

"He in there?" she had asked and he nodded.

They never spoke any more about that night. Everybody just figured the old man had got drunk and started the fire, probably with a cigarette. And for fourteen years Jackson had listened to stories about Maudie's ghost.

But now their talk was turning again to the new ghost. Jackson shook off the troubling memories and listened. He didn't have anything else to do.

"No, this wasn't like Maudie's ghost," Lonnie explained. "It was shaped like a man—like him. Wasn't it, Howard."

Howard shrugged. "Well, I didn't really get a look at it, just a glimpse out of the corner of my eye. Maybe it was like Griff says, just a shadow or something."

The other men looked from one to the other exchanging nods.

"I mean we had been working like the devil trying to get that grave filled before the rain set in, and I had sweat in my eyes and. . ."

"I 'spect every man workin' at the sawmill Friday will have a hard time shakin' that last image we had of him," Taylor offered. "Seein' a man split open by a saw like that. . . . Well, it just ain't somethin' we're likely to forget. And you boys were there so close to him."

"You saw him, Howard. I saw your face go pale. You saw him same as me."

Jackson started to ask who they saw or what, but a lightning bolt streaked across the sky and thunder cracked.

"Where'd that come from? Ain't it late for a thunder storm?"

The air that had grown deathly still, smothery almost, was shattered again by a streak brighter than the first, and an ear-shattering crack of thunder was followed by heavy sheets of rain.

Griff jumped to his feet. "Lord-a-mighty, boys, we'd better get inside a-fore we get fried or washed away."

Lonnie, Howard, Clark, and Taylor rushed to the door that Griff held back almost against Jackson's crate. They pushed by him and let the door swing closed without waiting for Jackson.

"Hey, you bums, I'm..."

"Jackson, let's go." The voice came from behind him. Let's go, Jackson. You got nothin' more to do here."

Maudie Houchins held out her hand and beckoned for him to follow her through the rain.

Never After
Jessie Grayson

Born and raised in Harts, WV, Jessie Grayson grew up in the heart of the southern coalfields. She is a wife and mother and believes that although life in the coalfields is never easy, it is always rewarding. She is currently working on a full-length novel.

Lucy carried on her mother's business with pride, the label of local soothsayer with less enthusiasm. She was not ashamed, only disheartened at how dividing it was. People liked things uncomplicated and ignored her military service and business degree, seeing only the witch.

She stared across the parking lot, past her truck, and into the mountains. The autumn browns of decaying leaves, mud, and naked branches spanned the distance. Shadows moved in the hollows, inky and wide. A few pedestrians stepped around her, seemingly oblivious of the leaping darkness. A trick of the weak light, she thought. But it pulsed as though alive.

"Lucy?" a familiar voice asked.

She turned to look at Jackson, and he removed his ball cap to rub thinning hair. A nervous habit her father inherited from him.

"How have you been?" he asked.

"Fine." She smiled. Her grandfather always made her smile. He reminded her of Daniel. She suspected that was the same reason he couldn't smile at her. "And you?"

"Good, fine." He scraped the toe of his boot on the asphalt. "I was wondering if I could hunt some around your place."

Lucy tilted her head. "Sure."

"Maybe I could stop by, for coffee or something."

She shrugged. "Watch for other hunters. I heard shooting at the old mine last night."

"I'll take a look, make sure they weren't messing around."

"There's nothing down there they can hurt."

"Still." He replaced the cap and shoved his hands into his coat pockets. "We're having a singing convention next week. I'd like you to come."

He told the truth, but her smile faltered. "Hate to think I'd make anyone uncomfortable."

"Everyone's welcome in the Lord's house. He set the rules there."

He waved as she got in her truck and drove away. Preacher never fails, Lucy thought as she drove. He caught a lot of grief over inviting her to church, but he still did. Shame, as her grandfather, he couldn't do the same with his own house.

As she went further away the road began winding, and she started gaining speed. Susan would never allow it. Lucy doubted the woman knew he spoke to her on those rare occasions. Turning a sharp curve, she saw a man standing in the center of the road and slammed her brakes.

Tires squealed and her truck scooted to a halt. Lucy watched him crumble, falling onto the asphalt. She scrambled from the cab, running toward him. "Are you all right?"

He sat hunkered, drawing long legs to his chest. "I wasn't hurt."

"You don't look so good."

He ran his hands over his face. "I haven't slept, showered, or eaten in two days."

"You're standing in a blind curve. Are you suicidal?"

He looked at her for the first time. Lank, greasy hair framed a lost face and mirroring eyes. "Not yet."

"Then get out of the road." Lucy took his arm, helping him to unsteady feet. Around his neck, a set of battered dog tags clinked, and she saw the thin BB chain. "You have a name?"

"Chance."

When they reached the side of the road, he pulled free and sat.

Lucy looked at the tag chain and remembered the weight of wearing them. "You need a ride?"

"I don't have anywhere to go."

She took his arm again. "Sure you do."

***

Lucy lived in a small cabin three miles off the nearest rural route and half a mile up a mountain. Chance sat on the couch looking out the window across the horizon. He hadn't said much, and she didn't ask. After a hot shower and some reheated leftovers, he looked sleepy, and she set a cup of coffee on the table in front of him.

Without turning he asked, "Who are you?"

"Lucerne Hayfa. Call me Lucy. I'm the local witch."

"A witch?"

She leaned against the door to the kitchen. "I see lies, and the truth of them. Got it from my mother."

He shifted, hesitating before meeting her gaze. "I stood in that curve because my dead wife told me to."

She nodded. "Yeah."

"She's trying to kill me."

"Maybe she was trying to lead you."

His eyebrow twitched. "I thought you would know."

"It only works if the person telling the lie knows it as a lie, or believes it as the truth." She smiled and he glanced away. "Why would she want you dead?"

He turned back to the window. "You got a nice view."

"I like it." Lucy watched the sky fade from grey to black, it seemed darker than normal, and she drew a breath to ask Chance but shut her mouth at seeing him asleep.

She sat at the kitchen table to sketch designs for border etching when footsteps sounded on the porch. Yawning, she moved to the door and remembered Jackson. She opened it with a smile that turned stiff.

He brushed in and looked down at the drawings, then at her. His voice crackled, a dark film covered his eyes. "Unholy circles brought forth evil."

She kept her back to the door, cold pouring into her stomach.

He glanced down the hall where Chance rose from the couch and strolled to the kitchen. Her grandfather stared as a snake would a rat before biting before setting his distorted gaze on her. "I've seen what you did and will stop it."

Lucy swallowed a thick lump in her throat. "What?"

He moved toward the door.

Stepping behind him to close it, she saw his body tense and his weight shift. She jerked her hands up as he grabbed for her neck.

Kicking his leg to no effect, she jerked a knee into his kidney, but he slammed her against the door and pushed an arm against her throat.

A shout and the sound of feet pounding filtered through her ears and Jackson darted away, Chance after him.

Gasping on the floor, Lucy felt dizzy and her chest ached.

"He's gone," Chance said at the door. "You hurt?"

"No." She rose to her feet and moved to the hall. A shelf fell with the racket, spilling pictures, books, and large terrain maps. She sat in the floor and starting picking things up to hide her shaking hands.

"Let me see." Chance knelt beside her and touched her chin.

Lucy pushed him away. Unrolling a paper, she put a picture frame on the corner. "Property maps my mother made."

"Okay."

"Look." She pulled another map with the same outline. The same property, but instead of landmarks grey patches dotted it.

Chance pointed to the map. "It's what she saw maybe."

She rubbed her forehead. "Lies wouldn't show up on maps."

"What do lies look like?"

"Darkness." She frowned. On the left-handed side, the whole map turned black and a passage written in sprawling hand said, *It seeks for you to destroy to feed. Perfect light can see through absolute darkness, but no one is perfect.*

Chance tapped a section. "What's there?"

"A rotting shed and old hand dug mine." Lucy drew a breath, the area Jackson went. She drew a large circle. "This is walking distance from here. I'll check it out in the morning."

"Why?"

Lucy shrugged and lifted the photo. The map rolled up, but she looked at the smiling faces. The woman's mouth was open with a bold laugh and her wide eyes looked toward the sky. The man, slight and nervous, stared at the woman with a grin.

"My parents," she said, catching Chance looking.

"They look happy."

"They were." She sat at the table and pointed at the passage on the map. "That is a warning."

Chance slid into a chair beside her. "She warned you about a lie in the mountains."

"Mountains don't lie."

"What else do you see?"

"Nothing." She swirled a cup of cold coffee.

"Maybe she saw something else."

"It doesn't work like that."

Chance held his hands up. "I admit to not knowing how it works."

"She believed a lie was darkness to the soul." Lucy stared at the picture. "There was a myth about women in my family being born to share the weight of truth. 'The moon is a light in darkness, and through the darkness it sees the world's truths.'"

"You don't believe that?" Chance said it as a question.

"It's an old story, excuses for psychic abilities."

Chance tapped the map. "No one is perfect."

"No kidding." Lucy moved to the fridge. Through the window, a shadow crossed the porch.

She ran across the kitchen and jerked the door open. Figures armed with shotguns skirted at the edge of darkness. A bottle slammed at her feet and fire splashed across the porch, but she felt no heat. Arms circled her waist and hauled her back.

Chance dropped her, slamming the door. "Where's the back door?"

Smoke crept through the walls, and she sniffed but didn't smell anything. "Don't have one."

Chance covered his mouth. "We have to get out."

"My bedroom window."

They squeezed through the opening and ran into the woods barefoot and cold.

***

Lucy ignored the crunching frost that burned her feet. She couldn't see where they were going, though she knew where they were heading. Behind her Chance kept pace, repeating the same question every few minutes: "Where are we?"

"Almost to the creek."

Chance stumbled over a log. "The creek that leads into the mine?"

Lucy stepped around him down the mountain. Slick leaves tangled her numb feet. "Something is wrong with Jackson, and it has something to do with that mine."

"Lucy, he burned your house. We need to call the police."

"Something is influencing him." She slipped and caught a sapling. "He wouldn't do that."

"You're not being serious."

She turned to him. "You stood in a blind curve under the influence of your dead wife's voice in your head. Was *that* serious?"

His hands balled into fists. "You don't know what you're talking about there."

"And you don't know what you're talking about here." Lucy pressed her palm to her forehead. "You know what, you don't have to go. Over that ridge there's a road—"

"No, you're not going alone." Chance cleared his throat. "Besides if. . . you're right, she isn't angry."

"What?"

"I was across seas when Rebecca died and when I found out—" Chance leaned against a tree and let out a shaking breath. "I could hear her. 'Walk,' she says, even when I was asleep. It got so loud, until I started walking."

Lucy chewed the inside of her cheek. Sometimes nothing said could make it better; the truth was hard like that.

"Kept walking, then she says 'Stop.'" Chance shut his eyes. "I'm in a curve with a vehicle coming. When I start to move she screams, 'Stop.' I thought she wanted me dead. Nearly fainted when you managed not to kill me."

Lucy met his eyes when they opened. "What's she telling you now?"

"Hasn't said anything since." Chance shook his head. "If you're right, if this is real, then she was leading me and wasn't angry."

"What if I'm wrong?"

"Then I walked around for two years out of my mind, and I just walked back into it."

"Let's go." Lucy turned toward the valley and he followed.

***

"Why is it so quiet around old house seats?" Chance asked.

Under the moonlight a stone chimney stood like a totem worshiped by weeds. Lucy followed the stream toward the shack. Weather-beaten walls slanted, and she started through the crooked door.

"We need a light." Lucy turned and scanned the mountainside. More than night lurked here and it would be watching.

"Careful what you wish for." Chance pointed toward a bend in the valley.

Headlights shone and a truck rolled into sight. With nowhere to hide, Lucy touched Chance's arm and he took her hand. The truck stopped and a figure emerged. She could see the long shadow of a firearm through the glare.

"Do not suffer a witch to live." Jackson's voice boomed as he moved closer.

"You really want that to be what it comes down to between us?" Lucy asked.

Again, she saw dark fog over his eyes. "Susan was right you're a worker of chaos, just like your mother."

"You don't believe that." She shook her head and felt Chance's hand tighten around hers.

"She stole him from us, stole him and killed him." Jackson worked the slide on his shotgun. "Just like you killed them."

"The accident killed him." Lucy heard her voice rise, anger burning her neck and cheeks. "And she grieved herself to death. You dared him in your house, and he died believing you hated him."

The fog faded a bit, tears brimmed in his eyes. "My only child."

She let Chance's hand go and reached for Jackson, but the emotion crumbled from his face.

He leveled the gun at her. "I have to save them, kill you to save them."

Cold surged into her chest. "Run!" Lucy sprinted around the mountain, feet pounding behind her. Chance pulled her to a halt behind a rock cliff.

"Where's the mine?"

Lucy looked where they hid. Halfway down a large indent cut into the rock wall. Rusted tools and buckets sat at the walled up mouth. The old bricks had cracked, and in the center of what looked like buckshot patterns, a few were missing. From the gaps, long tendrils of smoky darkness writhed over the bodies of two young men. "There."

Chance put a hand out when Lucy took a step. "What are you going to do?"

A shot rang out and whistled by them.

Lucy grabbed a shovel head. "Bust it open and hope it gets him first."

Chance drug her to the ground as another shot whined closer. "What happened to 'He's not normally like that'?"

Her chin quivered and she bit down to stop it.

"Think about it, Lucy. Maybe it's telling him what he told you."

She looked at the men covered in blood but saw no wounds. "You think it's lying to people?"

"You tell me. Is it? Maybe to feed? Isn't that what the passage said?"

The dirt in front of them exploded with a gunshot.

Lucy scrambled upright. "One way to find out."

Hefting the shovel head, she started toward the worming wisps. A thought occurred that if the moon's revealing light came from the sky, then why couldn't a deceiving gloom come from the ground.

"You're not perfect." Chance ran after her. "You can't stop it."

She slammed the shovel against the brick. The dull hit broke a large chunk and she smashed it again. And again until thick, cold air burst free. Lucy dropped the shovel and covered her face.

A roar split her head, filling her ears. Thousands of pleading, threatening voices merged into one ear throbbing growl. Darkness sucked all light away. Lucy's knees shook. Coppery blood filled her mouth and she knew that in the empty vacuum nothing could escape.

Tears burned her eyes. No one could reach her here. No one cared enough to even try now. Her head swam, the darkness swelled, and her legs failed.

Someone caught her.

The voices faded and in the void, a flicker appeared. The truth sparked.

No *one* is perfect, no *one* can see through absolute darkness. But two can. Even the moon must have the sun to shine.

The flicker turned to an inferno and the choking fear lifted letting her catch a breath.

"Are you all right, Lucy?" She saw Jackson pull her from Chance's grip. He sent a territorial glare over her head.

She got wobbly feet under her. "Are you?"

He rubbed his neck, then his side. "Feels like I just woke up from a nightmare or a bar fight. What happened?"

With the dazed effects vanishing, she managed a grin, and then glanced back at the men. They were not bodies, but alive and coming around. "Small cave in, looks like. We heard the noise, came to check it out."

"I'll... get the truck." Jackson frowned but turned.

Tired, Lucy sat on the ground to watch the hunters wake up. The gaping mine stood empty and silent.

Chance plopped down beside her. "If Rebecca did lead me here, can you tell me why?"

"No." Lucy looked up at the sky and the stars came into focus. "What made you think to grab me?"

"You fell and I caught you. Think she wanted me to save you?"

Lucy shut her eyes. The moonlight felt warm and a cool damp smell carried from the creek. "Maybe she wanted me to save you."

He leaned up and grinned. "Maybe."

***

Jackson dropped the two hunters off at the hospital, and offered to drive Lucy home before returning to check on them. Lucy rode in the middle, tapped her fingers in the uncomfortable silence, and listened to the tires hum on the road. He let her and Chance out at her driveway and rolled the window down. "Whatever happened tonight, I think I owe you an apology and thanks."

"Sure." She waved, starting up the mountain.

"Invitation's still open for next week. I'll save you a chair."

Lucy watched Chance walking ahead. Jackson was too alone to risk alienating Susan but maybe she could bend a little for him. "Save two, we'll see you there."

A broad grin cracked his face and he pulled out.

Halfway up she caught Chance and he smiled. "I think you're right. She led me here, to help me."

Lucy stopped. Darkness spread around him, a wonderful image of help and recovery, but on the inside sat the horrible scene of a fatal traffic accident. Chance believed Rebecca wanted to save him.

A lie, and at its center, the truth.

It's Failing Time
Miranda Phillips Walker

Miranda Phillips Walker spent her youth growing up between Fayette County, West Virginia, and Myrtle Beach, South Carolina; finally moving to Baltimore, Maryland, to finish her degrees in psychology and nursing. Miranda now makes her home in Charleston, West Virginia, and is an ER nurse at Charleston Area Medical Center. Her first novel, "THE WELL MEANING KILLER" was released in 2008. She is currently working on the second book in that series, while juggling a career, four children, and her husband, Robert W. Walker, a suspense and horror writer.

I consider myself a level-headed, realistic person, but after eighteen plus years in the nursing field, I can say, I have changed my tune when it comes to believing in ghosts, spirits, apparitions, spectral mists, haints—whatever you want to call them. Having been schooled in the scientific field, I always believed in logical explanations. That there was a logical reason for anything people would get up in arms about. You know, seeing ghosts walking corridors, seeing objects fly around, and my favorite: the light at the end of the tunnel. "Yeah, right!" Summed up my attitude. That was until it happened to me.

It was a little after eleven on a muggy, hot July evening in 1992 when I started making patient rounds from room to room. A new nurse back then with less than a year under my belt, I was nonetheless sure of myself most of the time. While all my nurse friends went right into the emergency room or the ICUs, I thought it would be smart to gain knowledge in medical surgical nursing (med-surg) first.

Plan was to then pick a more advance unit later. . . once my feet were wet. So here I was at Mercy Hospital on 3-West feeling great about it all and no clue to its being a big mistake.

Mercy 3-West, as it turned out, was more a glorified nursing home than the exciting field of nursing I had trained for. Worse yet, since I was the newbie on the floor, I drew the short straw and had gotten reports on the hardest, most difficult patients. Just the same, I squared my shoulders and walked out of the report room like it didn't matter, but of course my feelings were crushed. Anyway, I made my way down the hall to room 312 nervous as hell because I had never taken care of a ventilator patient before.

"Hello, Mr. Ross? I'm Melinda. I'm gonna be your nurse until seven in the morning."

No answer. My first thought was a question: is he dead? But I saw the gentle rise and fall of his chest, breathed easier myself, and went about writing his vital signs off the monitor. I was adjusting the head of the bed when I heard a loud crash that startled me.

"Oh, my gosh, what was that?" Chills had run up my spine, and I just stood there unable to move.

In a ratcheting voice, Mr. Ross asked, "Don't-cha-know what that means, young lady? And you're spose to be a nurse on this floor. You are a nurse, aren't ya?" The frail man from beneath the white sheet was staring at me like I was an idiot.

Snapping out of the fog I was in, I looked him square in the eyes and pointed over to the floor across the room. "Yes, sir. Just that the clock fell on the floor."

"Well, ya know what that means, don't-cha? 'Bout what will happen tonight."

I crinkled nose and brow. "Whataya mean? Things just fall. I'll call maintenance to fix it." I was trying to remember after taking report on ten patients if I had noted the man was confused or not.

He waved me off as if I were daft. "You must be new here."

"Yes, I am, but it's not a big deal. The clock'll be fixed." By now my face was flushed down to my neck, but the room felt suddenly and noticeably cold.

"It means there'll come three deaths tonight." His voiced had grown as chilly as the room.

"OOO-K, Mr. Ross, I'm sorry but you must be confused, dear. It was just a clock that fell, nothing else." In training, we were discouraged from entertaining such ramblings, so I grabbed the clock off the floor, placed it on the sink, and left the room for my next patient. Something about what he'd said upset me. . . unnerved me in fact, but I let it go and started off for my next patient.

The empty hallway told me that the other nurses were busy checking on their patients. Luckily, no one to read my agitated features. On the way to my next patient's room, I was reviewing her chart when somebody ran by me, nearly knocking me down, and then she jumped up and ran across the nurse's station counter and desk.

"Hey, you can't do that! Get down from there, now!" I bellied up to the end of the desk where this young woman was standing there crying. She looked to be in her thirties, was dressed in her own night gown, with both her hands around the front of her neck.

"What's the matter with you? Can you breathe? Are you choking?"

The woman had released the grip on her throat and was now sobbing into her hands. I was shaking but managed to say, "Please just stay there. I'm not going to hurt you, OK?" As I moved toward her, she kept moving away from me. Of course, there wasn't a darn soul to help me, a fact I learned after looking up and down the hallway. I turned back around, and she went running off into room 313 and shut the door.

"Where're you going? Come back here." I heard furniture scrape across the floor. "She's barricaded the door." I thought about it and there was no way out, I had to go ask one of the other nurses for help. I feared they would make fun of me, but a patient life might be at stake.

I raced back down to B-hall but found no one. Where was everyone? *On break? Eating? Smoking?* I poked my head in a couple of rooms, trying to imagine where everyone had gotten off to. I ran back down to 313 to find the door still closed tight. I then knocked.

"Hey, listen, I just want to talk with you. Please open the door."

Not a sound. I tried to push the door open, but it was stuck. I could feel the tears running down my cheeks, cursing the day I had even picked this stupid career, when a loud alarm sounded. "Oh great, now what?"

I headed back to the desk just in time to see Gloria, Charge Nurse for the night, hustle a crash cart into room 315. She was in such a hurry to get into the room that she nearly ran over a visitor to get in, and suddenly, I recognized the visitor.

It was my younger sister, Karen. I almost shouted, "Wait, what're you doing here?"

Karen was talking to the doctor and not answering me. *Why is she so upset?* I wondered. If Karen was here, then the patient in 315 must be someone we both knew. My mind raced, heart pounding, and I'd had enough. I didn't care who knew how distressed I was at this point, not my sister, not this doctor, and not the nurses; I wanted to know what in the world was happening, so I rudely stepped between them and grabbed my sister's hand. Well, almost. I tried but I watched instead as my grab for her wrist went right through Karen's obvious absence of flesh and bone.

I felt instantly frightened and queasy. I repeated the action three more times before I understood, before I got it. The truth left me feeling weird, cold, and fuzzy headed. I closed my eyes tight, and when I again opened them, I found myself floating above the patient in the bed in 315—above the body, staring down on the patient only to learn that I was looking at myself.

This whole sensation was overwhelming. I could see my sister talking to the doctor at the same time that the nurses and doctors were coding my body. *I- I'm dead,* I thought, *or else I'm in that awful dying state I'd chosen not to believe in all this time.*

"Wait, I'm not ready to die! What happened?"

"Told-ja there'd be three deaths tonight, newbie."

I looked toward the corner of the room only to see Mr. Ross and the lady in the white gown who'd run from me; the two of them were free-floating upwards, lingering at the ceiling now alongside me. I said to them, "You guys're dead. But this can't be. I just saw you, Mr. Ross, in your room, and her in the private gown in the corridor and at the station."

"Not too swift, are you, lassie?" replied Mr. Ross's apparition.

"At least your husband didn't kill you." The sobbing lady gestured to her neck, and I could now clearly see the red and blue bruising.

"No, but there's no reason for me to be dead. I'm healthy, young, I just started my nursing career." I looked down at the bed below to see the doctor listening to my heart, and I wondered why I could not hear it thumping away.

"Well now, dearie," began Mr. Ross' floating form, "something is amiss, or you wouldn't be able to see us, now would you?"

"Mr. Ross, when did you die? I was just in your room."

"My dear, I was already dead! Silly newbie. The ventilator was doing my breathing for me. Some nurse!"

"But you spoke to me!"

"Do patients on a ventilator normally talk?"

"No ... gosh ... I don't understand this. It doesn't make sense!"

"Perhaps our young nurse needs be ed-G-cated, Mr. Ross." The lady moved her hands to her hips.

"I don't need to be educated. I need to be alive!"

"Well now, we are not in charge of that." Mr. Ross took in a deep breath and let it out. "You see, my dear, after you took the report, you got dizzy and grabbed for your chest."

"Yes, yes, the other nurses hurried to get you into a room!" added the murdered wife. "They laid you down. Placed the cardiac monitor on you."

"How do you know all this if you're dead?"

"Yes I am a little dead, and it happened a little after midnight when I coded, and my nurse was working on me down the hall, and I was at the same point you are at this very minute."

A shiver rippled through my body where it lay on the bed. "What do you mean the same point?"

"She means you are not gone yet," Ross replied, "but you are in the process of, let us say *kicking the bucket*."

"Are all ghosts this mean?"

"Not mean, my dear, factual. You deal in facts, no? We are merely talking in the terms you understand."

"This is crazy. If I'm not dead, how can I come back?"

The lady and Mr. Ross looked at me then moved back, each pointing up. My gaze followed the direction they pointed at, and there it was! Crap no! Not the proverbial tunnel! But there it was, clear as window.

I felt the area around me growing narrow and dark, and yes, I felt drawn to the light. It was a mixture of brightness, with white and yellow colors, and I could feel this enormous pull on my body as it traveled upward.

"Don't fight it." I heard Mr. Ross's voice—muffled and far away. He'd gone.

There are no words to describe how fast and strange this experience felt. I was totally helpless to stop whatever was happening. As I traveled upward, the light grew brighter, but at this point, I finally opened my eyes wide. Then I saw the light in the background with several vague figures standing there. From all the accounts I had heard as a nurse, I knew I would be dead soon, as there was no turning back, so I just gave in or rather *up*.

There was a low-pitched sound permeating the air, and at the same time, I could hear the nurses, the doctor, and my sister talking.

"I'm sorry, Karen," the doctor was saying to her. "We did all we could."

I mentally screamed: *Don't give up on me!*

The doctor added, "Has Melinda been sick or having any heart problems?"

"No, she was as healthy as a horse," my sister insisted. "Nothing, what happened? Please tell me."

"We can't really tell, except the other nurses said she became dizzy, and she complained of chest pain. I assume you will want an autopsy?"

"Of course, I just can't believe any of this."

"Was your sister from the United States?"

"Yes, why?"

"Well we tried to insert an NG Tube into her stomach, and she ripped it out, but after that, she spoke in three languages other than English. . . ."

"What, what languages?"

"Well, she spoke in native Gallic, Spanish, and French. Did she take language classes in school?"

"No, she hadn't any interest in foreign languages! I- I need to be with her now, alone, please."

"Yes, we are just going to finish up, and then you can sit by her, I'm really sorry for your loss."

I had been focusing on this conversation, heartbroken for myself and my sister as well as my friends, all of whom I'd miss. The light around me dimmed, and I looked back over to the people standing about my body; I felt defeated, but I tried to move forward toward Karen when I was stopped by a strange pressure. It felt like a wall yet I saw no such wall.

Crying now, I tried again to move forward, but being unable to do this, I felt a wave of fear wash over me. Now I could not move in any direction, and I feared maybe I wasn't good enough to go to heaven. The people in the light, those odd figures, seemed to be familiar, perhaps past relatives, and I could not make out the words, but they were definitely buzzing with conversation they alone understood.

"Please," I mentally shouted, "I can understand what you're saying, and—and I'm scared."

"It's not your time," returned a melodic male voice, and I felt a pressure pushing me back, pushing me down and toward my body there on the hospital bed.

"Wait, I don't want to die." My body smacked hard into the bed at that minute, and I heard my sister scream.

"Hey, get the doctor back! She's breathing!"

One of the nurses came over to the bed to comfort her even as she yelled for the doctor to return.

"Doctor Nash, get back in here! She's breathing!"

The hospital bed was soon surrounded by medical staff checking vital signs and getting lab work. Karen stood out of the way, not sure of what had just happened.

"Melinda, this is Doctor Nash. Can you hear me?" he asked.

"Yes, am I... Am I alive?"

"You most certainly are! How do you feel? Are you in any pain? Can you tell me your name? How many fingers am I holding up?"

"Mel-lin-da... Three."

"Can you tell us what happened?"

I looked up at the ceiling, no ghosts. I wondered if this had all been a dream, but I knew better. I could still hear Mr. Ross's voice rumbling around in my head; I could still see the bruises on the murdered woman's throat. What's more, I felt more alive than I had ever felt in all my years. I felt every cell in my body breathing in oxygen. Every inch of me, from head to toe, embraced life, and I called out for Karen who rushed to me and we hugged.

"I had a premonition," Karen said. "It told me to get here and fast and I did. I thought I'd lost you."

Karen didn't know that she had lost me for a short time. I wondered how well Mr. Ross and the lady without a name were doing now in the light.

Deep River
Jason L. Keene

Jason L. Keene was born and raised in rural Wayne County, West Virginia. Although he has since moved across the Big Sandy River to Kentucky, he will always consider West Virginia to be his true home. Jason invites you to visit him online at www.JasonLKeene.com.

"Come, follow me, and I will make you fishers of men." — Matthew 4:19

At one time, Wilson Frazier fished to forget. Forget the bills stacked high on his kitchen counter and the unstoppable effects of time that ravaged his aging body, but mostly to forget that he was alone. It took a kindred lost soul to show him that he fished to remember.

Wilson tossed his line out into the water. The blaze orange bobber at the end swam with the current for moment before standing upright. Against the groaning objection of his knees, he lowered himself to sit. Leaning back into the shaded embrace of the ancient oak was like a hug from an old friend.

"Just you and me again today," he said.

Wilson preferred it that way. The solitude allowed him to think. There were better spots; the fishing along this snaking section of the muddy river was notoriously bad, but his focus was never on catching any fish. This stretch of the Mississippi, where the water ran slower and wider, still and deep like a giant tub of glimmering molasses under the glare of the late-summer evening sun, held meaning—held memories.

Laying the rod across his lap, Wilson reached into the inside pocket of his fisherman's vest and retrieved his flask. He glanced down to admire the worn gold plating and ran his thumb across the engraving etched into the faceplate. It read:

> Wilson,
> For fifty years of happiness, and to an eternity more.
> Love, Norma

He unscrewed the cap and took a long pull, the familiar feeling of warmth crawling over him almost instantly. He tightened the cap and tucked it back into his vest pocket, close to his heart. Norma had bought him the flask for their fiftieth wedding anniversary. She would have never expected him to use it—at least not to this extent.

Wilson wiped at his eyes with the back of his hand, sniffed back hard to clear his head and shifted his focus back on the bobber. Nothing yet, not that he had expected anything.

Through the salty layer of tears still clinging to his eyes, he noticed movement off to the left. He shifted against the tree, looking over to see a figure approaching nearby. The person shuffled through the weeds in his direction, a fishing pole balanced up and over one shoulder, a burlap sack in one hand and a lantern swinging from the other. It was still over an hour until nightfall, but this man looked to be in it for the long haul.

Oh, no you don't. This is my *spot . . . our* spot.

The small man didn't acknowledge Wilson's presence until he was almost close enough to get whacked by the fishing pole laid across his lap. "Gettin' any bites today?" he asked.

"Best take it on down the river a ways, old timer," Wilson responded, his tone cold and defensive. "This here's my spot."

The man gave him a sad smile. "Just fishing through." He made no attempt to advance into the shade of the big oak tree that Wilson openly laid claim to.

"No fish here. This spot's bunk, anyways. You ought to try on up the river a ways. Supposed to be a bend up yonder that has a honey hole. . ."

"Already tried up there," the man cut Wilson off. "Ain't got what I'm fishing for."

Wilson studied the man. His dark brown skin glistened under the setting sun, sweat rings forming along the neckline and armpits of his stained white t-shirt. His clothes were ragged, his receding salt-and-pepper hair and goatee unkempt—the man seemed to give his appearance the same lack of attention that Wilson gave his own. But it was when Wilson settled on the man's eyes that he felt he knew him—yellowed globes lined with puffy red luggage. They were the eyes of a man that had seen his miles of a hard road. The defeated owned those eyes—only the haunted wore that look.

Wilson scooted over on the grassless patch of dirt beneath the tree. He pointed a finger out towards the northern edge of the muddy water. "Just fish out over that way, understood?"

The man walked over and sat down in the shade beside Wilson like a cautious runt awaiting retaliation by its pack leader for doing something wrong. He sat down his load. "Name's Jesse," the man said.

"Wilson. And I hope you don't plan on catching anything. I haven't had a bite here in years."

Jesse wiped the sweat from his brow and stared out across the dirty surface of the water. "Maybe you're just using the wrong bait."

***

It was after dark before Jesse revealed what he had in the burlap sack.

The fishing had went as expected, with Wilson reeling in his line every so often only to find a limp water-logged worm on the hook, replacing it with a fresh one, and then casting his line back out. Jesse had not reached for his pole once.

Only after Wilson had drained his flask did he begin rambling about his stint in the Korean War. Jesse had nodded at the right times, but for the most part remained silent. The conversation had turned to politics and religion, Wilson offering views that he'd not discussed with anybody in years. Again, Jesse nodded and smiled.

With an open ear waiting on every word and a belly full of bourbon, it didn't take Wilson long to turn the conversation to Norma.

"Norma gave me the best fifty years of my life," Wilson said, pausing to belch. "And then *it* took her away."

"*It* took her?" Jesse asked. "What's *it*, Wilson?"

Wilson raised a shaky hand and waved it out towards the rolling surface of the river. "River took her. Norma was coming home from visiting her sister about five years ago, back when that freak storm hit. You remember it?"

Jesse nodded.

"It swelled the river, broke the banks. She was coming down the old road back there," Wilson said as he pointed a thumb behind them. "And... and she hit a dip in the road that the water had raised up over. It... it just swallowed her up, car and all." Wilson waved his arms out wide before clapping his hands together and drawing them in close to his chest for visual effect. "They dragged this deep spot here a few times but never came up with nothing. Like the river just dragged her on out there and..." Wilson left the sentence hanging in the night air alongside the cadence of the crickets and chorus of bullfrogs.

He didn't fight the tears that came with recalling it all. Whether it was the alcohol or the understanding he felt in Jesse's presence, he wasn't sure and didn't care. It just felt good to tell somebody.

After hearing Wilson's stifled sobs wind down to sniffles, Jesse responded. "You ain't out here after catfish at all. And you're using the wrong bait."

For the first time that evening Jesse reached for his pole. A massive treble hook dangled at the end of the line alongside several large weights used to sink the bait down to the deepest, darkest depths of the river's muddy bottom. Then he reached for the burlap sack.

"I knew your story before you even said a word," Jesse said. "I could see it in your eyes... could see that pain."

Wilson watched as Jesse removed an old, worn teddy bear from the burlap sack. Its tan fur was missing in sections, the remainder caked in dried silt and mud. One of the black button eyes had been pulled free and its left leg dangled limp and shredded, the stuffing emptied completely from the open cavity.

Wrong bait. Wilson watched curiously as Jesse sunk two of the three prongs making up the treble hook into the arm of the teddy bear.

"We had a flood like that many years ago," Jesse continued. "My daughter Lottie was swimming upriver with some friends down a side creek in the shallows when it hit. Came quick. Most of the girls got out of the water in time, but my Lottie got pulled down. They never found her either. But over the years, I did. Oh, they're strong down there in the mud after a few years, and they break off the line easy. They keep moving around with the current though, so you gotta' keep trying farther downstream." Jesse turned to face Wilson and his eyes were wide and wild. "And you gotta' use the right bait."

Jesse stood, reared back, and swung the rod sending the bear sailing out into the night sky. It splashed into the water, the line drawing tight as the weights dragged it down farther and farther into the black depths.

A chill washed over Wilson's skin as he watched Jesse's face tighten with focus, watched the man's fingers flexing against the tightened line of his rod waiting for a bite. *Is he insane?* The buzz that had swarmed around in Wilson's head drained away at the realization of the situation and he slowly began to reel in his own line. He had to gather his things without Jesse seeing, had to slink back to the road and get out of here. This old man was obviously crazy, but Wilson didn't intend on staying around long enough to find out whether he was dangerous.

Before Wilson could reel his own line completely in, he heard the buzzing spin of Jesse's reel. The line with the teddy bear lure shot out into the darkness with a fury, zipping one way and then the other, all the while a smile spreading wide across Jesse's face.

"Come on, Lottie! Come to Daddy, baby!" Jesse turned the reel to lock the gearing and the force of the sudden stop made the rod bend over double. The fiberglass flexed in the shaft, groaning under the strain, as Jesse's small frame leaned back against the hefty catch fighting on the other end.

Wilson wanted to run, to leave his tackle there and take off into the night as fast as his legs would allow. This was insanity. Surely a massive lunker of a catfish had ran across the teddy bear by accident, had been working silt along the bottom and inhaled the stuffed toy in the act.

Against his better judgment, Wilson found himself on his feet with his arms wrapped tight around Jesse's waist.

Whatever was on the other end pulled even harder in defiance of the added tension of Wilson's weight.

The two men slid as their feet fought for purchase along the mud of the river's edge. Jesse's hand turned the reel with slow and deliberate revolutions. The rod began to splinter at the middle.

"*No*," Jesse said through clenched teeth. "Not again. . . I won't lose you again, Lottie!"

Wilson was losing his grip around the man's waist, the two of them having nearly been pulled to the water's edge when the catch broke the water's surface several feet out. Wilson gasped as he looked around Jesse's waist at the abomination.

A head and shoulders surfaced, thrashing and churning the murky water into a bubbling stew, barely visible at the edge of the lantern's lighted reach. The thing's hair was dark and matted with greasy mud, the skeletal eye sockets void and black, and dark gray skin dangled in loose strands from the bones protruding beneath. Its maw was wide, the hinge of the jaw hanging open. A terrible gurgling cry burst from within the thing's ragged throat that ripped through the night air. Across its decayed chest, it clutched the soggy teddy bear tight with both arms like a scared child.

"Oh, Lottie baby," Jesse said between strained sobs.

And then Wilson's grip failed sending him back hard against the ground. He rose up on his elbows and watched in helpless horror as Jesse was dragged forward into the water by what could have only been his own daughter, the dark river swallowing him slowly from his ankles to his waist.

Deeper until the water was at Jesse's chest.

. . . at his neck.

Jesse was laughing and cheering when his head disappeared beneath the water's surface. Bubbles billowed up from farther out in the water.

Wilson stared out into the darkness at the water—afraid to move, afraid to breath—for what felt like eternity. The remains of Lottie had submerged once more into the dark depths. Jesse, too, was gone. The bubbles had ceased. Silence fell on the riverbank giving way to the crickets and bullfrogs once more.

***

Wilson Frazier waited until the next night to return to the bank of the murderous Mississippi River. He walked by the light of Jesse's lantern, and for the first time since losing Norma, he smiled. The aching in his joints no longer affected him as he found his worn patch of earth below the ancient oak with ease.

Wilson passed it and moved farther downstream.

He reached into his vest's breast pocket, close to his heart, and pulled out his flask. It was still empty from the evening before, and wouldn't Norma be proud to know that he no longer needed the alcohol to cope?

The crickets and bullfrogs sang and it sounded so calm, so serene. Their tune reminded Wilson of the song he and Norma had danced to at their wedding.

Just been using the wrong bait, that's all.

Wilson tied the flask that Norma had given him below the large treble hook and weighted sinkers at the end of his line. He gave the inscription one last look. He sighed and ran his thumb across the worn words.

And to an eternity more...

He stepped up to the muddy edge of the mighty river, to the spot just downstream of where Norma had been taken from him years before, and cast his line out for the last time.

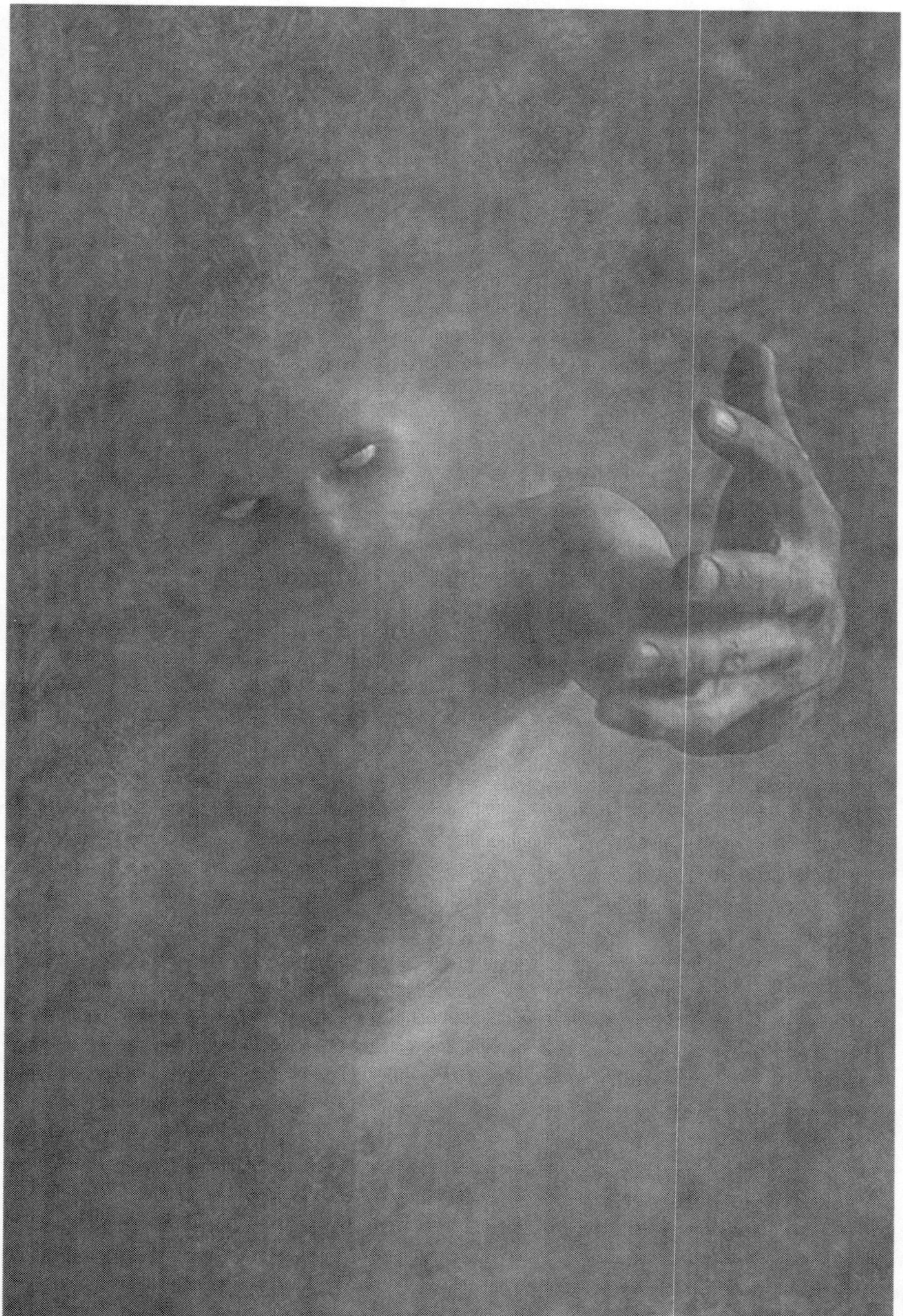

Thank You

Thanks to Woodland Press, LLC —Keith, Cheryl, and the whole gang—for your love for West Virginia authors and Appalachian subjects. Thanks to the contributors in this anthology for taking the time to participate. A special thanks to Geoff Fuller and Brian J. Hatcher for editorial assistance. Also, thanks to Tomasz Wasilewski, artist extraordinaire, from Poland, for providing the exceptional cover art.

VISIT
www.woodlandpress.com
for more information on your favorite
Woodland Press authors and book titles.

118 Woodland Drive, Suite 1101
Chapmanville, WV 25508
304-752-7152 • FAX 304-752-9002
Email: woodlandpressllc@mac.com

© Copyright 2010. Each of the contributors in this volume own the individual copyrights to his or her work, but each has given Woodland Press certain literary rights making it possible to assemble their writings, along with others, in this title, *Dark Tales of Terror*.

Other Great Titles From

WOODLAND PRESS

www.woodlandpress.com

Edited by Michael Knost
Foreword by Rick Hautala

Legends of the Mountain State
Ghostly Tales from the State of West Virginia

This anthology includes thirteen accounts of ghostly manifestations, myths, and mountain mythology, based on known legends from the eerie state of West Virginia. Horror writer Michael Knost serves as the anthology's editor. Participating writers are an amalgamation of professional authors and professionals in the horror, science fiction, and fantasy fields, along with up-and-coming writers from Appalachia. Many contributors are National Bram Stoker Award winning authors currently in the national spotlight. This title is suitable for anyone who enjoys bone-chilling ghost tales told by some of the best storytellers in the business. In its 5th printing. Softcover. $18.95

Edited by Michael Knost
Foreword by Gov. Joe Manchin, III

"This is one excellent read."
— Joe R. Lansdale

Legends of the Mountain State 2

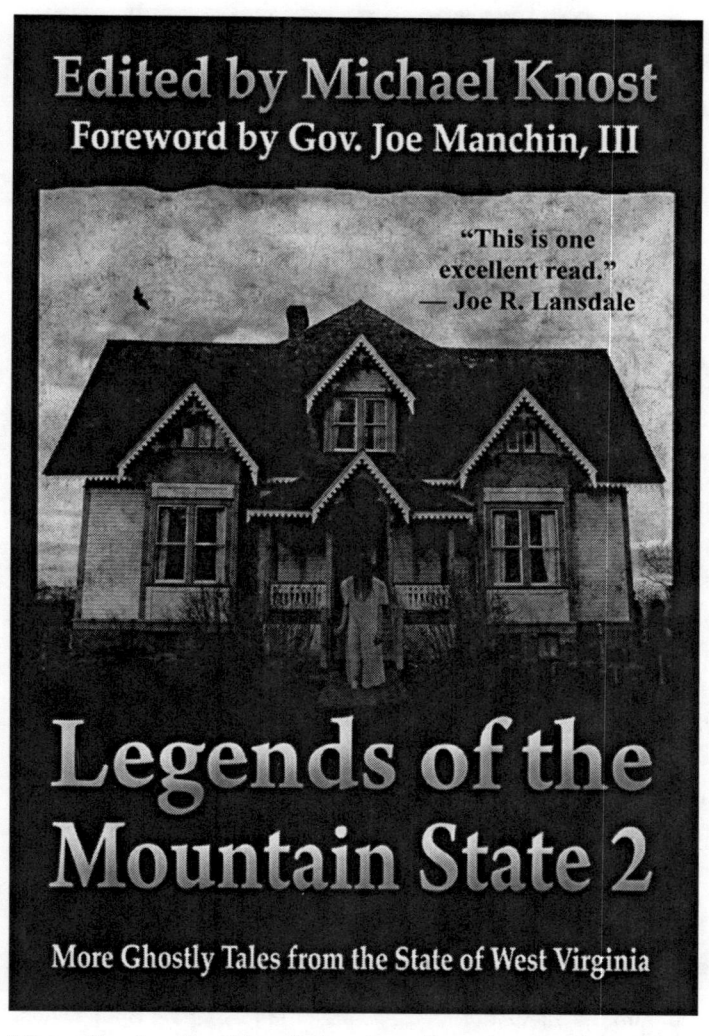

More Ghostly Tales from the State of West Virginia

After putting together this anthology's predecessor, editor Michael Knost realized he had barely scratched the surface with Appalachian folklore. After seeing great success with the initial project, Woodland Press asked Knost to put together a second edition—one that focused on 13 additional ghost stories and mountain legends. The new project, which is arguably even scarier than its predecessor, embodies the same tone and texture of its forerunner, with nationally known authors and storytellers getting involved. According to Knost, this new volume offers fresh meat to those who devoured the stories in the first volume. Softcover. $14.95

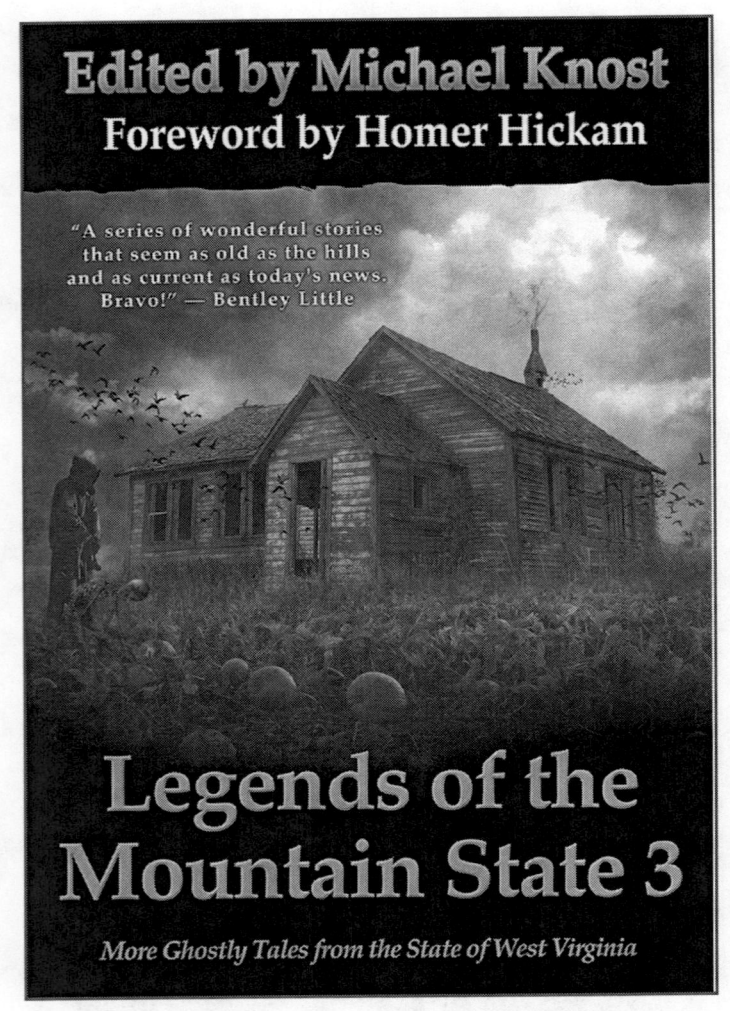

> **Edited by Michael Knost**
> **Foreword by Homer Hickam**
>
> *"A series of wonderful stories that seem as old as the hills and as current as today's news. Bravo!"* — Bentley Little
>
> # Legends of the Mountain State 3
> *More Ghostly Tales from the State of West Virginia*

The third installment of the *Legends of the Mountain State* series, above, is already being called the most amazing of the ghostly trilogy. Michael Knost again takes the reins as chief editor and coordinator. Here you'll find 13 final chapters—bone-chilling ghost tales and treacherous legends. Stories are penned by many of the preeminent writers in the business—National Bram Stoker Award winners, nationally known horror writers, and gifted Appalachian storytellers. The tone in this project is perhaps darker, tales creepier, and the overall texture even grittier than the first two installments. Foreword by beloved American author Homer Hickam. Order *Legends of the Mountain State 3* today. Softcover. $18.95

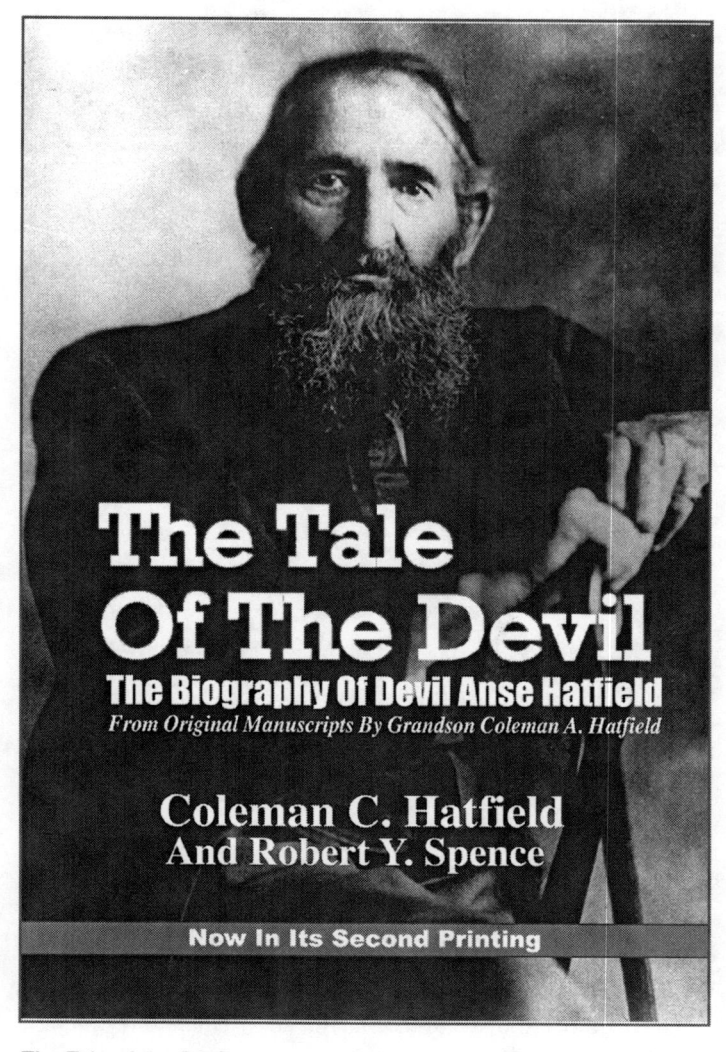

The Tale Of The Devil
The Biography Of Devil Anse Hatfield
From Original Manuscripts By Grandson Coleman A. Hatfield

Coleman C. Hatfield And Robert Y. Spence

Now In Its Second Printing

The Tale of the Devil represents the first biography of feudist Anderson "Devil Anse" Hatfield, written by great-grandson Dr. Coleman C. Hatfield (2004 Tamarack Author of the Year), and Mountain State historian Robert Y. Spence. Now in its third printing, this book remains an Appalachian bestseller. This biography of Devil Anse Hatfield faithfully documents his Civil War service as a Confederate soldier and leader of the fighting Wildcats militia, and tells the true story of the Hatfield-McCoy feud, the violent killings, and the post-feud years after the fighting ceased. Handsome Hardbound. $29.95

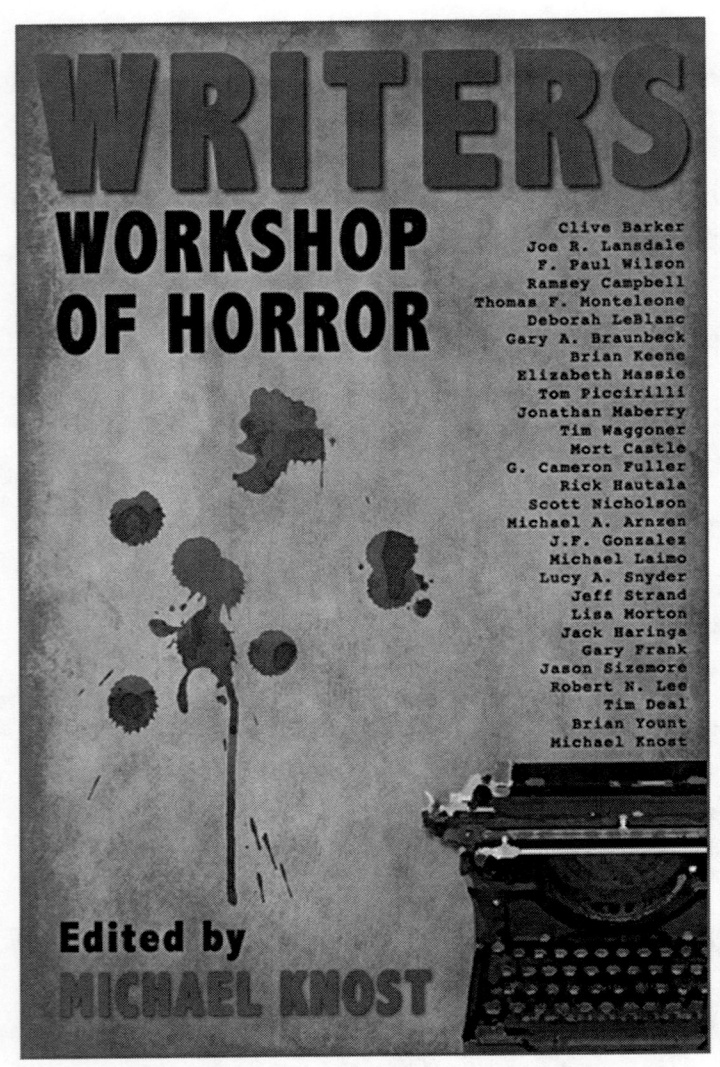

"Packing more knowledge and sound advice than four years' worth of college courses... It's focused on the root of your evil, the writing itself." — *Fangoria Magazine*

BRAM STOKER AWARD FINALIST. Contributors to this work include: Clive Barker, Joe R. Lansdale, F. Paul Wilson, Ramsey Campbell, Thomas F. Monteleone, Deborah LeBlanc, Gary A. Braunbeck, Brian Keene, Elizabeth Massie, Tom Piccirilli, Jonathan Maberry, Tim Waggoner, Mort Castle, G. Cameron Fuller, Rick Hautala, Scott Nicholson, Michael A. Arnzen, J.F. Gonzalez, Michael Laimo, Lucy A. Snyder, Jeff Strand, Lisa Morton, Jack Haringa, Gary Frank, Jason Sizemore, Robert N. Lee, Tim Deal, Brian Yount, and others. Softcover $21.95

Winner of the Black Quill Award

Appalachian Case Study: UFO Sightings, Alien Encounters and Unexplained Encounters. The state of West Virginia has a prominent history of unexplained happenings and bizarre sightings of unidentified flying objects (UFOs). This fascinating literary work researches and documents sixteen unusual UFO sightings in Appalachia. The book also includes fascinating interviews with certain West Virginia citizens who have experienced the unexplainable. Author Kyle Lovern includes an exclusive interview with nationally-known and respected UFOlogist and nuclear physicist Stanton Friedman. This title has received a great deal of national attention as the focus on UFO data shifts toward Appalachia. Softcover. $12.95

FEATURED ON COAST TO COAST AM with George Noory. Appalachian Case Study: UFO Sightings, Alien Encounters and Unexplained Encounters - Volume 2. In this new release from Woodland Press. which is a sequel to a bestselling title about strange UFO sightings and bizarre alien abductions, UFOlogist Kyle Lovern focuses and broadens his scope as he researches and fully documents a variety of new UFO encounters, and revisits some famous sightings of yesteryear, that have taken place in Appalachia—in West Virginia, Virginia, Kentucky and Ohio. Softcover. $15.95

WEST VIRGINIA TOUGH BOYS
REVISED EDITION

VOTE BUYING, FIST FIGHTING AND A PRESIDENT NAMED JFK

F. KEITH DAVIS

Foreword by WV Senate President - Lieutenant Governor Earl Ray Tomblin

West Virginia Tough Boys. A regional bestseller, *West Virginia Tough Boys* remains a historically significant literary effort about mountain politics and the 1960 presidential primary campaign in the state of West Virginia. Rich and straightforward stories of political tomfoolery, vote-buying and eventual victory for Senator John F. Kennedy in the Mountain State's primary are documented here, as well as the making of a Mountain politician. West Virginia has often been sited as the most important and vital win in Kennedy's original bid for the White House. The book features indepth interviews and discussions with a variety of politicians and campaign workers from yesteryear. Softcover. $19.95

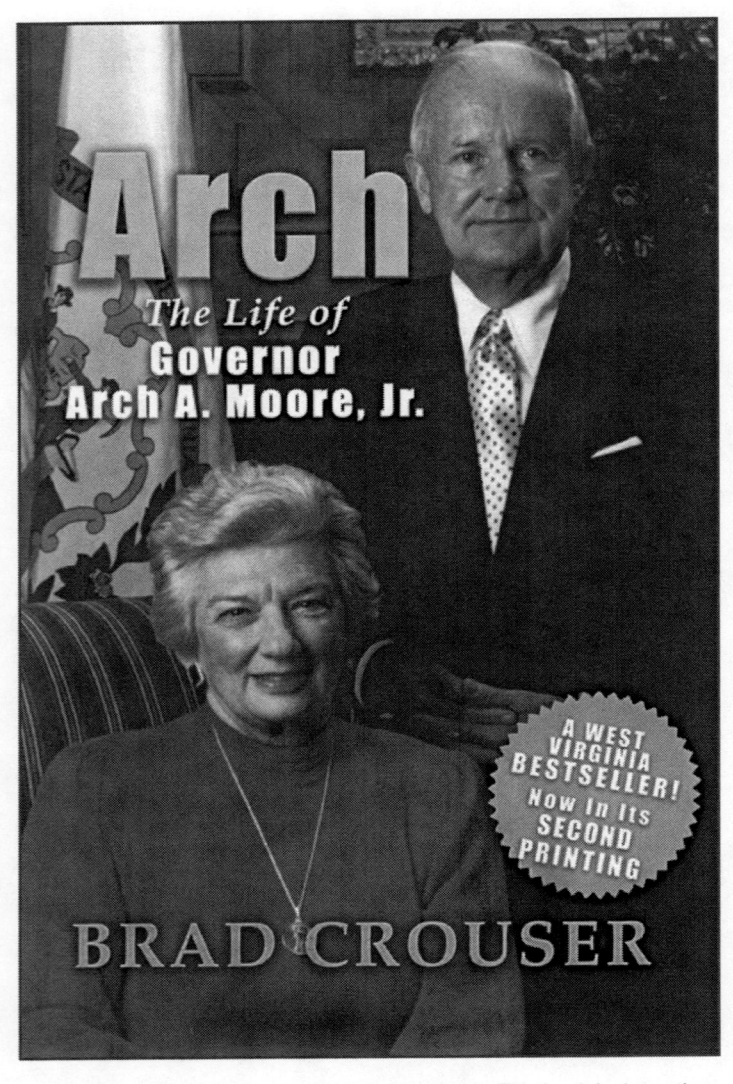

ARCH: The Life of Governor Arch A. Moore, Jr. This book is the authorized story of West Virginia Governor Arch A. Moore, Jr. Author Brad Crouser, a Charleston lawyer and former state tax commissioner, takes the reader on a fascinating journey, from the turn of the Twentieth Century and Arch's grandfather, the entrepreneur F. T. Moore, to the present day of his Congresswoman daughter, Shelley Moore Capito, from the mountaintops of triumph to the valleys of tragedy. Now in its second printing, this volume should be in every personal library. 612 Page Softcover. $32.95

The Secret Life and Brutal Death of Mamie Thurman. It was over seventy-eight years ago that this nasty homicide grabbed national headlines. This book takes a close look at this puzzling account. A regional bestseller, this book has been dubbed the "Hillbilly Dalia." It's a gruesome thriller and true account about a prominent, Depression era woman—a carry-over from the flapper age—found brutally and sadistically murdered in the heart of the Bible-belt. It was the last year of Prohibition. Mamie Thurman was a member of the tight-lipped, local aristocracy that frequented a private club in downtown Logan, WV—a wild speakeasy. She lived a risky lifestyle. Now new evidence points to several groups—from the mob to the KKK, from rumrunners to a slew of local merchants—as having a part in this true-crime. Softcover. $15.95

The Feuding Hatfields & McCoys. This unique book is about two proud families. *The Feuding Hatfields & McCoys* is a title that includes a comprehensive timeline of the feuding Hatfield family migration westward and documents the history before, during, and following the bloody feud era. Included are stories—which have never before been published—that have been collected from the Hatfield family over the years. These chapters add color and clarity to this famous vendetta. Author Dr. Coleman C. Hatfield was the great-grandson of Anderson "Devil Anse" Hatfield and was a noted Mountain State historian. Softcover. $18.95

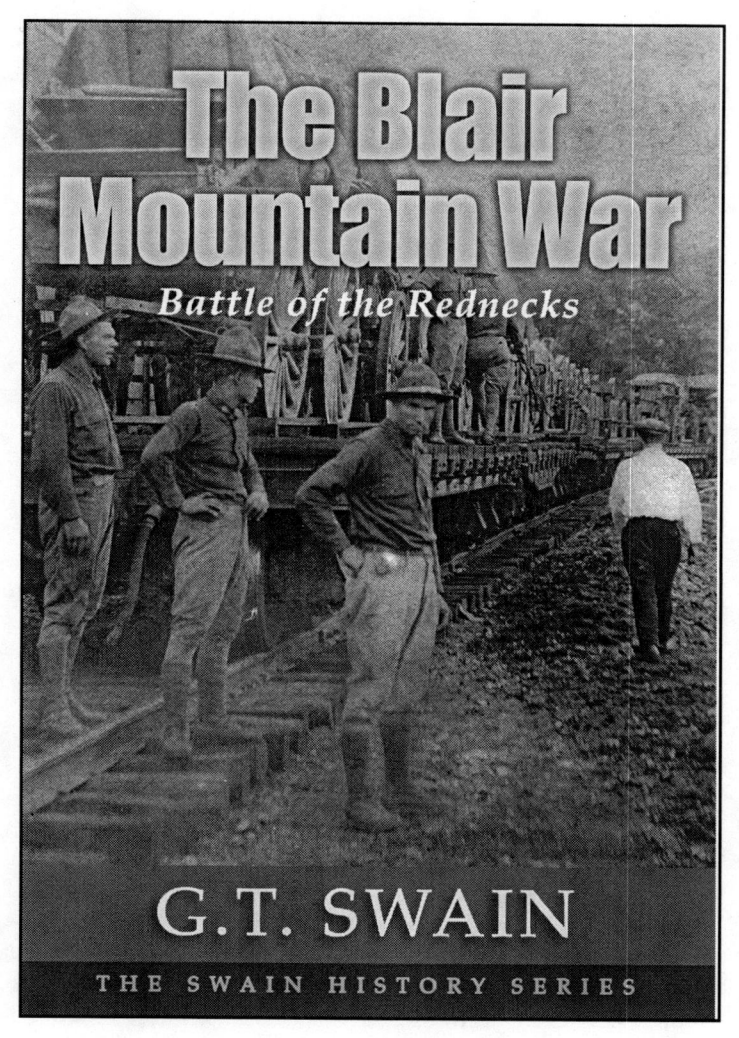

The Blair Mountain War: Battle of the Rednecks, tells the true story of the Blair Mountain War, the largest organized armed uprising in US labor history. At the time of this original manuscript, written in 1927, G.T. Swain was a reporter for The Logan County Banner, in Logan, WV. Here Swain paints a vivid picture, in his most unique style, and documents the accounts surrounding the 1921 Blair Mountain War. The WV State Archives has since stated that the mine wars have demonstrated the inability of the state and federal governments to defuse the situations short of initiating armed intervention. This is certainly true. Regardless, the details behind The Blair Mountain War remain fascinating and controversial. $12.50

Princess Aracoma and the Settling of West Virginia. Upon the tragic death of Chief Cornstalk in 1774, the Shawnees followed Cornstalk's daughter, Princess Aracoma, into present-day Midelburg Island in Logan County, West Virginia. This book aptly describes the settling of the Mountain State and explains how Princess Aracoma resolved a difficult conflict between the American Indian population and the region's earliest settlers. This title was originally authored by journalist and historian G.T. Swain in 1927. The end result is a true story and an exciting adventure, involving Indian Princess Aracoma, that takes place upon the immense backdrop of American history. $12.95

VISIT
www.woodlandpress.com
for more information on your favorite
Woodland Press authors and book titles

WOODLAND PRESS, LLC
LOGAN PUBLISHING HOUSE

118 Woodland Drive, Suite 1101
Chapmanville, WV 25508

Email: woodlandpressllc@mac.com